[redacted]

THE BARISTA

To Believe is Not Enough.

Elijah G. Clark

[redacted]

FIRST EDITION

Designed by Elijah Clark

The Barista
Visit website at www.TheBaristaBook.com

Printed in the United States of America

ISBN: 1-62209-249-X
ISBN-13: 978-1-62209-249-9

This novel is dedicated to my sons Malachi and Elisha.
I pray that this story always comfort you with
peace and purpose.

Table of Contents

INTRODUCTION

Rather than love, than money, than fame, give me truth.
—Henry David Thoreau

The Truth:

Subconsciously, the average person gets caught up in their own system of life and direction. We choose ourselves as god by following our own rules and believing in whatever feels good. With society praising creators and disparaging followers, we have inevitably found ourselves clutching onto what is new rather than traditionalism. That way of life has transitioned into our spiritual walk, and we have created false prophecies and customized biblical doctrine to our liking. Believing in God is considered old truth, while magic and fate have become the gods of the new age. Worshipping Christ is no longer an honor, but it has become a separation of those who praise and those who desire worldly approval and position.

We've configured our minds to believe that because sinning is natural, then it must be right. We are afraid of believing because we fear following blindly and giving up control. We no longer try the spiritual route because we desire independence from all law that doesn't approve of our free mind. As our desires hold firm to this world, following is looked down upon and is considered acceptable only for the weak-minded.

Even those of us who do claim to love Christ, don't do much to show our love for Him. We simply expect that whatever our mouths proclaim, our hearts and spirits will also feel the same. We have little understanding of anything outside of our day-to-day. While God is the God of Heaven, Earth and all of the stars in the sky, we have belittled Him down to a mere fairytale. We've created Him to be a figure in which we believe we can simply accept, and we do nothing to validate our love and dedication toward Him.

Somehow, we have convinced ourselves that we can make it to Heaven by just repeating scriptural text that we don't truly understand. We pray and claim faith, but we do nothing of action to become worthy of God's gift. We tell ourselves that we can make it beyond this world if we just wait in silence. The fact, according to scripture, is that something must be done in order to show our love toward God. We cannot do nothing and expect everything in return. The reality is that in order to love God, we must do as He desires. Love and doing are one and the same. If we love Him, then we should desire to change out of what is natural and transform our minds from its sinful nature.

More than anything, we should seek to know truth. Truth isn't in a book, temple or through the words of another. There is nothing that can be said or done in order to find it. Truth is a feeling and understanding within yourself that is gained only through a personal relationship with God. Most of us get distracted away from truth as we turn our attention toward religion instead. Instead of using religion as the tool it is, we grasp onto it as a crutch and follow the rules and rituals it creates.

What steers most of us away from truth is that we

don't know how to handle the peace that comes with truth. Many of us have become fearful of our own thoughts and judgment. We intentionally distract ourselves with chaos and drama in hopes that we can fall asleep at night with the sound of the television whispering in our ears. Our minds have become addicted to staying away from peace and introspection. We're losing the war in our minds because our spirit never gets time to talk to its Creator.

Our lives have become fixated with fiction, and because we are satisfied, we effortlessly follow the wrong paths. It has become almost impossible to find purpose. Easily, our minds break because we've been cracked and wounded our entire life. We're stuck in a system that dilutes our minds from truth and peace. We not only lack spiritual knowledge, but we don't even seek to know the truth of all truths.

Most of us aren't even aware of the consequences that are connected to our choices. Searching for a comfortable resolution, we attach ourselves to the one that requires the least amount of commitment.

Though our hearts may at times have an appetite for God's love, our minds often disagree. We continue moving in the wrong direction simply because it's easier than starting new. We seek truth in lies and close our minds to anything that takes us near the reality of our failures.

If we look deeply, we'll realize that the world holds no truth. Truth doesn't come from this world, but it lives in a world outside of this one. We don't have the power to control or create truth because truth existed before us. Therefore, we must learn to follow. In order to find truth, we must stop looking for it and start asking for it.

This book will help you get a better understanding of not only who God is, but also who you are within His world. You should have a better understanding of your purpose and position as you seek to follow Christ. Everyone has a position in this world. We are all purposed to do something of relevance according to God's plan.

While some of us may feel like leaders at times, we were born to be followers. We all serve something or someone even if we don't know we do. No matter what we do or say, there will always be Another greater than we are. We must not only believe in Him, but we must also follow Him as He desires.

Come journey with me through the process of becoming a true and desirable follower of Christ.

One
THE PREPARATION

You decide what you want to be truth.

I heard the window blinds opening and immediately felt the Sunday morning sun beaming on my closed eyelids.

"Get up, George. You have a plane to catch," my wife said, nudging me as she began cleaning the room.

I stretched my body in the warm white sheets before rolling over and placing my head under the feathered pillow. "I'm not going," I mumbled.

"Well, if you aren't going to work, then you can get up and come to church with Mindy and me."

I threw the pillow from over me and jumped out of the bed. "I'm up, I'm up!" I said jokingly, feeding into Carol's humor, as she knew I hated going to church.

"I thought so," she smirked.

I walked behind Carol while she organized the large dresser and wrapped my arms around her.

"Good morning beautiful," I said before kissing her on the cheek. "Are you going to miss me today?"

Smiling, Carol turned her head away from me before answering. "I'm for certain not going to miss your morning breath," she joked.

After I turned her around, we held one another briefly, until I slightly pulled her away and stared into her brown eyes.

"What are you thinking George?" Carol asked.

I continued to stare at how beautiful she was before replying. "You're still the same crush I fell in love with more than 9 years ago."

Carol smiled and then buried her head back into my chest. "I can't believe we've been married for so long."

A voice yelled from another room. "Mom!" Mindy shouted.

Carol pulled herself away from me. "There it is—the reality check. I now feel old again," she said smiling.

Placing her head into the hall, Carol yelled back to Mindy who was at the kitchen table. "I'll be down in a bit!"

Closing the door, she turned to see me staring in the mirror.

"Didn't you say your flight was at 10:30?" she asked.

I turned to look at the clock, which read 8:15. Knowing that I had planned to leave no later than 8:30 to take the 45-minute ride, I ran into the large closet that was through the bathroom and began searching for something to wear.

I grabbed a short-sleeved collared shirt and a pair of wrinkled blue jeans before rushing to put them on.

"I'll make it. As long as I have my bag checked an hour in advance, I'll be fine."

"You know how long that bag-check line can be. Why not just take a carry-on? It's only for one day."

"You know I always need my suit bag. I can't just cramp my best suit into a carry-on. Showing up to a business meeting with a wrinkled suit isn't a good look."

"Just iron it, like any normal person on a budget."

"That sounds like the solution of someone who enjoys ironing. I'd rather just bring the extra bag. It's all about personal convenience."

"Or laziness," Carol said. "Didn't you mention Steve was going with you?"

"Yep," I answered before turning on the loud automatic toothbrush.

After washing my face and fixing my hair, I went back into the bedroom, sat on the edge of the bed and began putting on my socks and shoes.

"Is Steve coming to pick you up or are you driving yourself?" Carol continued as she began getting dressed.

"We're both driving our own cars. He lives in the opposite direction of the airport— you know that. He never picks me up."

Carol's attitude became serious. "You two sure know how to waste money. Here we are trying to save, and you're just spending it on nonsense. I just thought you would be trying to save more and spend less carelessly."

"Well, it's too late now. Besides, this little trip isn't going to break the bank."

Carol walked over to me, sat down on the bed and then placed her hand on my shoulder before saying softly, "Why are you doing this? Why not just go and find another job somewhere else?"

"Not right now, Carol," I said getting up from the bed. "I don't want to do this today."

Disappointed, Carol got up and started making the bed. "Are you ever going to tell me why they fired you?" she continued. "What could you have possibly done by just helping churches market themselves?"

Frustrated, I threw my hands up. "Is that all you think it is? These churches only care about marketing so that they can make money. I don't help them with marketing; I help them to scam people. It isn't about God, church or the Bible."

Carol placed her hand on my back as I stood hunched over the dresser. "I'm sure that's not true, George."

"Well, you haven't been to a new church almost every week like I have. When I walk into these meetings, they act as if they just want more members so that they can expand upon the religion, but the truth is they only want more members so that they can collect more money from them."

I turned around to face Carol. "Tell me, when was the last time you've been to church and wasn't asked to come out of your pocket?"

Without allowing Carol to answer, I continued. "Church is a business like any other business. They're just selling a different product. Matter of fact, they're selling the best type of product: one that doesn't exist—the almighty magic God who has a floating Kingdom somewhere in outer space."

By now I was over by the window, staring out at the grass when Carol replied, "Are you serious, George? That's how you see God— as magic?"

"I'm not saying that, Carol," I said, knowing that she was sensitive about her religion. "You know what I mean."

"I only know what you say, not what you mean. You're talking absurdity," Carol replied angrily.

"I'll be downstairs," she continued. "Mindy should be finished with breakfast soon. Come down when you're ready."

After Carol left, I finished dressing and packing before heading downstairs.

"Hey Daddy," Mindy chirped when I walked into the kitchen.

I smiled when I saw Mindy eating her dark cereal. Walking over to her, I moved her short brown bangs from her forehead and gave her a kiss. "Good morning to you too."

"Your toast is in the toaster. Hurry up and eat before you leave. You have a few minutes," Carol said, putting away the bread.

Mindy got up to place her bowl into the sink. "Daddy, for my birthday I need a new bike. My old one is too small and I don't like those colors anymore."

"You need?" I questioned. "Either way, your birthday isn't for four months," I said, grabbing my toast and placing it on a paper towel before sitting at the table.

Mindy sat down across from me. "It's three months, not four."

"Okay, well your birthday isn't for three months. We just bought that bike two years ago."

"But it's too small now," she whined.

"Okay, Mindy. We'll see what we can do. How old are you going to be anyway? Four?" I asked jokingly.

Mindy grew upset. "Not four! I'm going to be six!" she said while expressing with her fingers. "I was three a long time ago."

"You're still my little baby. I like you better at five. I don't want you to turn six."

Mindy ignored my comment and continued. "I already know which one I want. Mommy said I had to ask you first."

"It sounds like you're asking me second," I said before turning around to Carol, who was smiling while rinsing Mindy's bowl.

I got up from the table and threw my paper towel away. "Okay, ladies. I have to get to the airport. Are you two going to be okay without me?"

"You going to Florida again Daddy?"

"Not this time, Minney. I'm going to California."

As I went to pick-up my briefcase, Carol grabbed my arm and pulled me into the dining room. "I haven't told her anything about you losing your job, but if your plan doesn't work, then we'll need to tell her something," she whispered.

"Tell her something for what? She's only five. She doesn't need to know about this. Don't worry about it anyway. Everything will be fine. If it doesn't work out, then I'll make sure to tell her if that will make you feel better."

"I'm just saying, George. We aren't in a good position financially right now. Is everything already paid for with this trip?"

"Yes, I told you yesterday. I still have the plane ticket and the room reservation. If they cancel the room, then I'll just have to use some of our money, but it will be worth it, I promise. I'll get a ride with

Steve around the city, so there's no need to worry about that."

"I can get a job if I need to," Carol said with hesitation in her voice. "This is why we shouldn't be relying on one income anyway. This is what happens. I can get a desk job somewhere, maybe even start working at a daycare again. Mindy is older now and she doesn't need me full-time any longer."

"No, Carol. You don't need a job. You have to trust me. There's always somewhere for me to work if this doesn't pan out. I can go back into selling cars if I need."

"You know that's unreliable, George. You have to build up new clientele, and that can take months. We've been living paycheck-to-paycheck for the last few months trying to pay off my student loans and your hospital bills. Our account will only hold us 'til maybe next month."

As Carol stood worried with her head down and tears streaming down her face, I wrapped my arms around her and held her. "Everything will be fine," I assured her. "I just plugged myself into God this morning."

Carol laughed and then playfully hit me in the chest. "You know you're stupid, right?"

Carol and I took a deep breath to calm ourselves before we walked back into the kitchen. I grabbed my luggage and gave Mindy a kiss. "All right, I'll see you two tomorrow night. Be good," I said before giving Carol a kiss and heading out the door.

After arriving at the airport, I realized I didn't have any time to drop off my car at the long-term lot, so I parked in the garage and headed into the airport with a little over 20 minutes before I needed to have my bag checked.

While waiting in the slow moving baggage line, I thought about what Carol said about just taking a carry-on. I realized she might have been right. With the line being so long, I was afraid I wouldn't make it.

Oddly, not only was the line going slower than normal, but only half the usual number of agents were working.

Nonetheless, despite the slow line, I arrived to check my luggage with no time to spare before I ran toward the security line.

While waiting in line, an announcer came on the intercom for the airline and announced that my flight was boarding.

By the time I made it through security and to my terminal, the doors were being shut for my flight. "Wait, wait!" I yelled while running toward the ticket counter and thrusting my ticket at the woman.

"You just made it," the woman said as she scanned my ticket. Another agent opened the door and I ran down the walkway to the airplane.

After arriving to my seat, I saw Steve was already seated with his attention out the side window which he was sitting next to.

As I sat down on the aisle seat, I placed my luggage in the open seat between us.

"Hey, George. What are you doing here?" Steve said with a puzzled look. "I thought you got laid off on Friday. Everyone has been talking about it."

I shrugged. "It was just a misunderstanding."

Confused, Steve continued, "Are you sure? Jim has already told everyone about the next step and who would get your clients. He said they'd be handing them out tomorrow."

"Are you serious? They fired Craig and Joe last month and they got their jobs back. I'm better than them. They never handed out *their* leads."

Steve shook his head.

"I'm not worried. I'm just going to play this meeting out and go from there. Everything will be okay."

After getting situated in my seat, I asked Steve, "I know they might call you tonight, but don't tell them that I'm here until after the meeting, okay?"

"Of course, George," Steve assured me.

"Do you want to check out my part of the presentation?" I asked, before opening my briefcase.

A male flight attendant walked up to me. "Sir, please secure your items under the seat in front of you. We're about to take off."

"Oh, sure," I responded. "I'll show you the presentation later," I said to Steve before putting away my briefcase and buckling my seatbelt.

As the plane took off and before the captain turned off the seatbelt sign, I continued to think about what Steve said about the company giving away my clients.

"Are you sure they said they're giving away my clients tomorrow?" I asked Steve.

"Jim said it and Paul was there with him. It seemed pretty serious to me."

Steve took out his laptop and practiced his pitch.

I continued thinking for a moment before turning to Steve, who was busy reading and whispering the lines of his pitch loudly.

"You've been doing this for more than seven years. You should have a majority of that speech burned into your memory by now."

Steve chuckled before responding. "I thought I was going to this meeting by myself, so I included your part also. It took Paul and me three additional days just to do the research. And it's different for everyone. I can't use the same pitch for all of the clients. I might use some of the material, but most of it is unique to the church. You know that. You've never heard me use the same pitch."

"I guess so," I said before recalling the church debate I had with Carol earlier. "Carol and I almost had an argument about church this morning,"

"Oh," Steve said with a concerned look before placing his laptop down. "What was it about?"

"Nothing big. She just doesn't see it like I see it. We just have two different views on it."

"I see," Steve said, placing his hands on top of his laptop and fading into thought.

"Anyway, check out my pitch," I said enthusiastically.

I opened my briefcase, pulled out the printed document and handed it to him.

Steve skimmed through the document, nodded his head and handed it back to me. "Looks good."

"You don't want to read it?" I questioned.

"I trust you know what you're doing, George. You don't need my approval."

As I placed the pitch back into my briefcase, Steve turned toward me and asked, "What did you and Carol almost argue about?"

"Nothing big," I shrugged. "She can't accept that the Church is a business that's out to make money like everyone else. I'm sure you know the truth just as I do. You've seen it enough."

"Seen what enough?" Steve asked.

I pulled my Bible from my briefcase. "This," I said holding up the perfectly bound tan and brown leather Bible. "You know just as well as me that this is just a bunch of garbage that's used to trick money from innocent people. Churches are all about *selling* Christ. I know you've seen it also. Every church I submit a marketing plan to only cares about that one thing."

I saw the disagreement on Steve's face. "C'mon, Steve. You and I are some of the top consultants within the industry. We're probably the best if you seriously think about it. We're salesmen. We don't actually need to believe in what we sell. We only need to know the material. We just help promote churches to consumers. You can't actually sit here and say that God really exists. He's just a marketing pitch; just merchandise that churches sell to achieve their financial support."

Steve shook his head in disagreement before putting his tray up and placing his laptop under the seat in front of him. "Are you being serious right now? Is that how you look at what we do?"

"Of course. Think about it. Look at all of the hypocrisies, riddles, damaged translations and corrupted people we work for and around. This religion thing is just a business, and Jesus is the product. Tell them what they want to hear. Find their trigger points by getting into their damaged hearts. Preach that success comes through dreams and security. That's it—That's all churches do. It's ridiculous to believe in this whole thing.

"They sell God like a car salesman sells a car. Get into the customers' emotions, find their weakness and then take their money. I learned that at the dealership where I used to work, and I've been using it for years as a part of my marketing plans that I pitch to these churches."

"You just don't know the truth, George. You're everything that you're calling the churches. Churches aren't selling to their members; they're offering guidance. You make your own choices. You decide what you want to be truth. However, to judge those who do believe in God as being fools, you're being offensive. Saying that churches are selling religion is like saying a teacher is selling education. Not only that, but you can't judge all churches based on only a few."

"Stop lying to yourself, Steve," I replied, squinting my face. "It's me you're talking to. I'm not going to tell anyone. Think about it. God sent himself down to Earth so that people could 'pick up a cross' and 'follow him to death.' He wants you to 'eat his flesh and drink his blood.' He loves you, but he hates practically everything you do. You'll never be good enough for him, no matter how hard you try. If you don't listen to or do everything he tells you, you go to Hell and burn for eternity.

"Does that sound about right?" I shook my head in an up and down motion hoping to get Steve to do the same.

I continued after not seeing him agree. "Being in a relationship with God sounds like a woman being in an abusive relationship. He'll beat you down, but at the same time, he'll tell you he hits you because he loves you. What a mighty and loving God you serve."

Steve put his head down in disappointment. "This is the reason Jim said they let you go."

"Did he tell everyone why I was fired?" I asked

upset.

"No, I just asked what happened, and he told me that you had stated to multiple customers your plan to gain them more money. A few customers even mentioned that you were stating God wasn't real. He said customers have been complaining about you since before the accident."

"I'm just being honest, Steve. You know you feel the same. I understand if you don't want to say anything because you don't want to lose your job, but you have to admit God isn't real. Religion is all made up by some extremely smart businessmen who now have millions of people wrapped around their political fingers.

"Either way, if the company needs me to play along, then I'll play the game with everyone else. I suppose I'll be just like the churches we market for. If they can act and tell stories for money, so can I. I'm going to be the best God-fearing believer you've ever seen," I said sarcastically.

"I know it may be hard for you to believe, George, but I disagree. Even if I didn't, you can't just go around telling churches that God isn't real and that all they are after is money. Most of us felt sorry that you lost your job after being back for only two months. We assumed it had something to do with the accident last year. Maybe you need a break. Maybe you need this time off to find yourself. You've been working too hard, and you haven't been the same since you came out of a coma. I can't imagine what you must be going through. If you want my suggestion, I'd say take the time off. Get yourself together and then find out what you truly want to do."

"Sure, Steve," I said disgruntled, realizing I wasn't going to get him on my side.

After the conversation, Steve and I didn't speak to one another for the remainder of the flight from Virginia to California.

After landing at the airport and exiting the plane, I headed toward the baggage claim and Steve went for the airport exit. "I'll be over getting the rental, George. I'll be back to pick you up," he said before heading toward the glass doors near the baggage claim.

Thinking that Steve was upset, as I waited for my bag, I continuously looked outside, not knowing if he would return. After my luggage arrived, I waited outside of the airport on the sidewalk, hoping that Steve would show up. I waited more than 20 minutes, which was much longer than he usually took to get the car. Looking around the entrance and parking area of the large airport, I got more nervous as each minute passed. I knew he could have easily called the job and told them that I was with him. If he did, they would have probably told him to leave me and go on with his work.

Getting more worried by the minute, I continued waiting until a blue sports car parked in front of me. "Get in," Steve said.

Relieved, I rushed into the car without putting my luggage in the back seat. I didn't ask why he was so late, because I didn't want to stir up trouble, and I was sure he knew he didn't have to come back and get me.

"Is the meeting still at 7:00 tonight?" I asked, trying to get comfortable with my briefcase and suit bag on my lap.

"Yep," Steve said while focusing his attention on

finding the airport exit sign.

"Do you want me to go first?"

"Of course. Let's keep it like we always do. You open and I'll close," Steve said enthusiastically, allowing me to become more at ease.

I sat in the passenger seat looking out the window and at the scenery before Steve interrupted, "Do you still have your hotel room or did the company cancel it?"

"I actually don't know to be honest. I should have called. I guess we'll see once we get there."

As we arrived in the large lobby of the hotel, Steve and I went to separate agents to check-in.

"How can I help you today, sir?" the woman at the counter asked.

"Yes, I have a room for George Henry. I'm here to check in."

"No problem sir. Could I please see your I.D.?"

I gave the woman my driver's license and as she checked the computer, I waited nervously.

"I'm sorry, sir. I see that you have a cancelation that was placed yesterday morning. Is that correct?"

"Yes, it's fine. I didn't know if I would make it or not. Could you please get me another room if you have any?" I handed her my debit card. "Put it on this card."

Giving the woman the card almost crushed my spirit. I had already spent money on the car garage and the luggage. I didn't know how I was going to explain the additional charges to Carol. I had thought about asking Steve to let me sleep on his room floor for the night, but I didn't want him knowing about my financial issues.

Steve finished checking-in and then walked over

to me. "How's everything going? Are you okay?"

"I'm okay. You can head up now if you want. After I'm finished here I'm going to go over my notes and relax for a bit."

"Okay, sounds good," Steve said, and then patted me on the shoulder. "Meet back down here at 6:00?"

"That'll work."

After I finished checking-in, I went to my room and rested on the bed for a few minutes before I called home and left a voicemail to let Carol know that I had arrived safely.

For a few minutes, I paced back and forth in the room and went over my pitch notes trying to perfect them for the meeting. I knew I had to do a good job if I wanted to ask for my job back.

With 20 minutes before I needed to meet Steve in the lobby, I went into the bathroom, washed up, put on my suit and stared at myself in the mirror. "You need this, George. You'll get this. It's easy. It's already done," I said aloud, hoping to motivate myself before the meeting.

I finished primping, cleaned up and then met Steve downstairs. After we arrived to the car, he asked, "So, what's your plan for today? Are you planning on going into this meeting and coming out with your old job? How did you see this day playing out?"

I paused and reflected for a moment before answering. "Well, the first part played out like I thought it would. Now I just need to go and blow this pitch away. If the customers like my presentation and sign on, then I'll have a better argument to ask for my job back."

"Sounds good to me," Steve said unconvincingly.

As we pulled into the parking lot of the large church, we grabbed our briefcases and went into the huge white stoned building.

Arriving inside, I first noticed the bright lights within the lobby and then looked at all of the many auditorium door entrances ahead.

The dark-skinned concierge walked from the glass room on our side with a clipboard in one of his hands. "Can I help you two?"

"Yes, we're with the GM Group," Steve answered professionally to the concierge who was wearing jean shorts and a blue t-shirt.

"I only have one person who's supposed to attend this meeting," the man said while looking through his list. "Steve Mayer," he said before looking up. "Which one of you is Steve?"

"I'm Steve," Steve said and then showed the man his driver's license. He then gestured toward me. "This is George Henry. He should be on the list as well."

"There is a George Henry here, but he's crossed out. Someone on the day shift must have done it by mistake. You two can go through," the man said while staring at me with a look of suspicion. "Go down the hall there and make two lefts," he said, pointing down the hall to our left. "The room will be at the end of the hall on the right. The Bishop should already be in there waiting."

Relief came over me, having had made it in the door. I only had one more obstacle, which was to put together the best pitch of my life.

As Steve and I walked into the room, we saw the husky Bishop and three others waiting at the opposite end of the round table. Each was wearing their summer clothing and looked to have been having a humorous conversation before we walked in. Steve and I walked over to each of them and introduced ourselves before we got started with the presentation.

I pulled out my notes and handed each of the church leaders a report that showed their church's status within the community compared to their competitors.

I proceeded by starting with my presentation. "Thank you all for taking this time to visit with us today. We are honored to have this opportunity. Nonetheless, let me get right into it. The purpose of this meeting is to gather the appropriate information that is needed to help you fulfill your church's calling and purpose. We've come up with multiple ways that will not only help the church prosper and grow, but that will also improve how you affect and communicate with the people of the community.

"We have analyzed your needs and desires, and we've dedicated ourselves to designing an effective strategy that will undoubtedly ensure that your church is reaching its goals and—"

"Excuse me," a voice at the door interrupted.

When I looked over to see who it was, I saw that it was the concierge from the front.

As he stared at me and from the look on his face, I knew exactly what he wanted. "Mr. Henry, could you please come with me?" he said.

I looked over to the church's leaders, hoping that they would say something to allow the pitch to continue. When they said nothing, I turned to Steve who had a sympathetic look on his face.

He reached in his pocket. "Here are the keys," he whispered, handing them to me, "you can wait in the car if you want."

Silence filled the room as I shamefully grabbed my notes, put them back into my briefcase and followed the concierge out the building as he lectured me for lying my way into the church.

I went to the car and sat in the driver seat as all kinds of thoughts and emotions raced through my mind. Tears fell down my face when I realized that I had to tell Carol the terrible news. I didn't know what I was going to do to fix any of it. I had no plan. I had already begged for my job back, and had been looking for new work since before I was fired and couldn't find anything.

I pulled down the visor mirror. "You're a failure, George," I said staring at my soaked face and red eyes. "You're a weak, pathetic failure. You're an idiot for coming out here thinking that you could change things."

After taking a few deep breaths to stop myself from crying, I wiped my face and placed the car key into the ignition as I began flipping through the radio stations.

This is the largest earthquake on record to ever hit the country. If you are anywhere on the East Coast around the state of Virginia, then take shelter. If you know anyone in that area, call them if you can get through and pray for their safety.

Confused and in fear, I jumped up in my seat, grabbed my cell phone and dialed Carol. The call went straight to voicemail, and my heart nearly pounded through my chest as I thought the worse. I called the house and then everyone I knew in the area, but no answer from anyone. I considered getting up and going to get Steve, but without hesitation, I found myself driving toward the airport.

I sped down the highways and maneuvered my way through the congested traffic until I arrived at the airport. I parked the car out front and ran inside to the nearest ticket counter. "I need a ticket to Virginia," I said, gasping to catch my breath.

"Sir, you have to wait in line," the woman at the ticket counter said.

I banged my fist on the counter. "Just give me a ticket!" I yelled as the woman jumped back.

Hoping to control my anger, I calmed down. "Please, just give me a ticket. I need to get back to my family."

Before I could say another word, a man for the airline came over to the counter. "Can I help you?" he said in a deep voice.

I walked backwards away from the counter. "No, I'm fine," I said as I turned around to leave.

A rugged looking man with a large beard who was waiting in line grabbed my arm and I quickly turned around, pulling my arm away. The man put his hands up for me to calm before he responded. "There are no flights or trains going out for hours at least. If you have a loved one who was hit by that earthquake, you need to find another way back," he said.

I looked at the kind person and didn't say anything. My thoughts were lost in panic, not knowing what to do.

I ran back to the car, and the next thing I knew, I was driving down the highway for hours listening to the radio before I zoned out.

Two
THE INGREDIENTS

Do you have a reservation?

As I awoke, my eyes widened, and with only a split-second to react, I pushed my foot against the brake as hard as I could. The noise of screeching tires and a blaring horn filled my ears, while the colossal impact sent glass shattering and the airbag slamming against my face. I had dozed off for what felt like only a few seconds, but that was enough to veer me off the road and into the light pole, which the hood of the rented sports car was now wrapped around. While the horn faded, the car radio continued to play. I sat slouched over sideways, barely moving.

This is by far the worst earthquake that the United States has ever seen. Reports are stating that the earthquake hit somewhere within the state of Virginia. It's believed that many won't make it out alive.

As the radio died out, tears welled up in my

reddened eyes. I had been driving for more than six hours, trying to keep myself awake on the long trip from California back to my home in Virginia. Carol hadn't answered her cell or the home phone, and I couldn't get a hold of any neighbors, family members or local businesses. No one was answering, and all that I had were radio broadcasters keeping me updated with the latest information.

Struggling to sit up in my seat, I stretched my right arm to massage the excruciating pain that had been throbbing in my left shoulder. Yelling in anger, I fought the air bag from in front of me and then banged my fist against the ceiling continuously, only to soon regret the pain it caused.

The last thing I remember before drifting into sleep was that the highways were full of traffic from what the radio broadcaster said was caused by an accident.

Not wanting to be stranded in traffic, I took a back road and didn't find my way back on the highway for what I believed to have been more than two hours.

The little strength and energy that I did have left was wasted yelling and screaming. Pushing myself to fight through the pain, I refused to allow the accident to stop me from getting back home. Carol and Mindy were far more important to me than my own injuries and pains. A meager car accident could be nothing compared to what they must have been feeling after the earthquake. I could only imagine what they must be going through, possibly trapped under fallen debris, calling out for my help. There was no way that I could just leave them there.

My phone hadn't worked for the last two hours. I

had also been ignoring Steve's calls to save battery power. I was sure he had found out about the earthquake by now and knows why I left.

I continued to sit in the car, expecting someone to drive by and offer assistance. After waiting for what felt like 10 minutes and with a headache that was only getting worse, I felt there was no choice but to push through the pain and go in search of help. After opening my car door and trying to lift my left leg to get out, I realized it had also been injured and I could barely move it.

Pushing the car door farther open, I bent over head-first, placing my hands on the ground, and crawled my way out. Once my knees landed on the grass, I rolled over on my back and gasped for air. Somehow, that small challenge of getting out of the car was enough to help me realize how out-of-shape I was. I realized that there was no way that I could walk for long with only one fully functional leg and arm. Being without food and water since the plane ride, my body started to feel as weak as I knew it was.

I got up on all fours, held on to the car door and pulled myself up to rest my back against the car. Once I looked around, I realized that the accident happened on a curved road. That notion confirmed that the chances of me being found were unlikely. Not only that, but there were trees everywhere blocking my field of vision and blocking anyone in a distance from noticing my blinking emergency lights.

I looked down the road in each direction through the trees and could see nothing other than streetlights. No headlights, street signs, stores or gas stations.

Staggering to the front of the car to see the damage, I noticed a small cloud of smoke coming from under the bulging hood.

Limping back to the car door, I sat down in the driver's seat and changed the radio station to see if I could get a signal—but nothing. The radio died, and with no signal on the radio, the headlights dimming and the horn going out, I concluded that the battery was draining. Recognizing that I was stranded and too injured to walk, I decided to wait in hopes that a car would come so that I could ask for help.

I sat down in the driver's seat and rested before looking over to the passenger seat and noticing the small doll with blue hair that must have fallen out of my briefcase during the crash. It was Mindy's doll, which she always kept in my briefcase. The sight of it flooded my mind with memories and reminders of the robbery a year ago.

Emotions built as I remembered that one dreadful Saturday night. I've tried many times to forget, but news of the earthquake and thinking of my family in harm brought back a frightening reality. Six dead, among them a four-year-old girl and several others critically injured, including me.

I barely survived that nearly fatal gunshot wound to my chest. A wound that also fractured my fingers and left the lower part of my body temporarily paralyzed due to spinal shock.

That tragic night started when Carol and I decided to bring Mindy along on our monthly movie night. It was usually just the two of us, but Mindy had been asking all week to see the newest popular family film at the local theater. With all of the begging and Carol ultimately giving in, we decided to just make it a family movie night.

We left the house a few hours early as we

normally did so that we could stop by the mall and walk around. After visiting a few stores, we stopped in one where Mindy saw a doll she wanted, and we purchased it. It was supposed to do some tricks, but needed batteries. I told Mindy that I would get some after the movie.

Later, when the movie had finished, we decided to stop at a local mart to get a few late-night snacks before heading home. While at the checkout counter, Mindy interrupted just before I was about to pay the cashier because she remembered I had said I would get batteries for her doll.

Neither Carol nor I remembered which type of batteries it needed, so I went back to the car to check. I couldn't have known then, but that decision turned out to be a costly mistake that changed my life.

On my way back to the car, I had passed a group of young men who were headed into the mart. I hadn't known then, but those men were the gunmen that would leave me near dead and hospitalized.

While in the car searching for the doll on the backseat, I heard a scream coming from outside, and I whipped my head around to see where it came from. A woman outside was screaming and pointing to inside the mart.

I looked to see what she was pointing at, and my heart almost stopped when I saw the men inside pointing guns at the cashier.

Before I could think of anything to do, I was out of the car and heading for the mart. Beyond the screams and commotion, a loud gunshot thundered through the crowd that had formed outside. I looked to the front of the mart where the cash register was located and saw the cashier's blood splattered against the wall behind the front counter.

I knelt on the side of the mart next to a window, looked in and was able to see one of the four gunmen lining the customers up against the back wall. My eyes frantically scanned all around the store, searching for Carol and Mindy, but I couldn't see them anywhere. After a moment, I noticed one of Mindy's pink sneakers sticking out from one of the back aisles.

I went to the window in the back end of the mart nearest them, knocked lightly on the glass and failed to get their attention. Carol had Mindy cuddled within her arms, both with their heads down and covering their faces.

I easily found myself bent over on my knees crying. After pulling myself together and looking back through the window at Carol and Mindy, I was distracted by a shadow at the end of the long aisle. There, one of the gunmen stood watching shockingly. He ran down the aisle and grabbed Carol and Mindy. Without thinking, I got up, ran to the front door of the mart and went inside.

Walking with my hands up, I pleaded that the gunman let them go for my own life. Two of the gunmen yelled for me to get on the wall with the rest of the hostages. Even while cornered by the gunmen, I continued to plead and yell that they let them go.

As the gunmen remained distracted by me, another hostage snuck up from behind one of them and attacked him before being thrown up against the wall.

A shot was fired. The bullet missed the brave customer's head and perforated my chest instead. I continued to hear loud shots being fired until I finally passed out.

When I awoke three days later, the doctor stated that the bullet had entered my chest and came out through my back, but didn't fully hit my spinal cord. However, the impact of the metal, which was lodged in my body, triggered a spinal cord shock.

As I remembered that night and thought of the earthquake, tears continued to fall.

Still waiting in the car, I hadn't seen any other car come by in either direction. The roads were still completely empty and no headlights for as far as I could see. The accident happened almost an hour ago, and no one was yet to drive by. My thoughts were that most people were probably home watching the news and calling their loved ones. The people who were out were probably smarter than me and decided to stay on the highway.

Sitting and waiting didn't seem useful, so I decided to suck up the pain and start walking in hopes that I could make it to the main road. At the least, I could get back on a straight road or find a farm or business to get help.

I pulled myself from the car, shut the door behind me and staggered down the curved road.

When I approached the first light pole around the curve, I was exhausted, so I stopped to catch my breath. The 40-foot walk felt like hours of hiking. With my back against the pole, I focused my attention down the street ahead to the next street light that looked to be 70 yards away. The blinking light reflected on a small sign under it. I couldn't make out what it said, but based on my physical condition, any sign was a good sign.

Seeing the sign gave me comfort and new energy.

I stretched my arms and legs before continuing down the street. The closer I got, the better I could see the wooden sign. As I approached the light pole, I started to limp faster until I read aloud, "*A Taste of Heaven.*" I didn't immediately know if I should trust the painted white text on the dirty wooden sign.

I wondered what type of place it would be. With a name like that, it had to be a restaurant of some sort. I was confident they would have a phone or radio.

The arrow on the sign pointed down a dark dirt path, surrounded by trees and plants. I couldn't immediately see any lights or buildings.

While continuing to catch my breath, I figured it was either I go down the narrow dirt path into the unknown or keep going straight down the road, which didn't have any other signs in sight. I figured the sign had to have meant something was there. No one puts a sign up with an arrow that points to nowhere.

Realizing that I had nowhere else to go, I decided to follow the arrow down the dark path. A few steps later I began gasping louder and stronger, not because I was tired, but because I feared the sounds and the midnight darkness that had surrounded me. The trees arching above became overwhelming as they walled around the dirt path that was now fading to patches of grass. I had been walking for more than five minutes and hadn't reached an opening, nor had I seen any lights or path ahead.

The dirt path was now long gone behind me, and the night sky was only getting darker. Only the small rays of the moon's light peeking through the trees helped guide my way.

Beyond the sounds of my own footsteps crackling

the fallen leaves, I could hear chattering through the trembling tree branches. I stopped and held my breath, hoping to get a better sense of which direction the noises were coming from.

The sounds stopped for a moment before they came back faster and harder until the trees rustled and the ground rumbled beneath me. The entire forest felt as if it were caving in. I tried to accelerate and escape whatever large animal or beast that was following me. The sounds against my path grew louder and closer until I leaped and fell on the ground right as a tree came crashing down behind my foot, barely scathing my heel with its branches. The forest chattered louder, and I could hear all types of bellowing sounds along the forest floor. I stood up and ran, dodging branches and forgetting all about the pain from the accident.

I was lost and I couldn't go back now. When I felt I had escaped whatever sounds were following me, I knelt down on my hands and knees and caught my breath before looking up to see a sign that read *A Taste of Heaven.*

Seeing the sign helped me to realize that I must have been going in the right direction. I inhaled one last time before continuing toward the direction in which the sign pointed.

Another three minutes and I started to hear the sound of the wind whistling. I reached an opening with a small dried-up creek and short walking bridge. I stepped across the bridge and onto rocks resting on another dirt path.

I felt confident that I was going in the right direction. However, based on how far I had gotten from the site of the accident, I started to think that maybe I was headed in the direction of an old location that no longer existed. I couldn't believe, and it didn't make sense that anyone would walk that far or long to get to a restaurant or home even. Not only that, but perhaps the path itself was called *A Taste of Heaven.* Maybe there was no building. Maybe I was just on a simple bike or hiking trail of some sort.

I continued walking before approaching hundreds of hanging tree limbs that blocked the dirt path. I stopped and thought, *The longer I go forward, the farther I will be away from what I know.* It made no sense to keep going farther into the deep forest. I was hoping to get lucky and find help, but maybe it was a bad idea.

I questioned why I even started following the path in the first place. Maybe I should have kept going down the road where there were light poles. Maybe I should have never fallen asleep while driving. Maybe I should have stayed on the highway. I felt like I had made so many wrong decisions within the last 24 hours. My wife and daughter needed my help and here I was hiking in the forest.

I turned around to head back in the direction I came, but an aroma coming through the wildflowers and pine trees stopped me in my tracks. The smell grabbed my attention, and I turned back around. Once I moved a few of the hanging tree limbs, I discovered a red light blinking in the distance. I rushed through the trees, and after going more than fifty yards, I stepped out of the woods and was met with the strong smell of freshly brewed coffee. In front of me, bright red and white lights spun on a sign on top of a brightly lit restaurant that read *Diner.*

I ran to the building and knocked on the glass doors as hard as I could. "Hello! Anyone in there?

Please! Anyone!" I found myself crying, gasping for air and yelling all at the same time. I was sure that if anyone was in the diner, I might have scared them off. "Hello! Please! Someone!"

While I watched through the glass doors and windows of the diner, I could see someone coming out of the swinging red doors from the back and slowly walking toward my direction. The elderly man took his time walking toward me, and he first grabbed his hand napkin and note pad before answering the door. "Do you have a reservation?" the man asked.

I responded frantically. "Please, thank you so much. I was lost in the forest and I'm just happy to see you. Do you have a phone I can use? I just need to make a call. Please, I'm begging you."

The man stepped farther out the door and squinted his eyes to get a better look at my condition. I noticed he was wearing a nicely-tailored suit.

"Do you have a reservation?" he asked, as if he were unfazed by my sense of urgency.

While he stood with the door open, waiting for my answer, I tried to look over his shoulder into the empty diner to see if there was anyone else who may have heard me.

"I'm sorry for banging on your door. I don't want to eat; I would just like to use your phone so that I can make one phone call. My wife was in the earthqua—"

"Do you have a reservation?" the man interrupted.

"No, no, I don't have a reservation. I just—"

"Wait here." The elderly man pointed to a white bench outside next to the door.

As I stood at the glass doors that had now been

shut in my face, I watched as he went back behind the swinging doors of the diner into what I assumed to be the kitchen.

I'm sure he doesn't get much business with the lack of customer service he has. A restaurant like this can't get many reservations, I thought while waiting outside.

I looked around the front of the diner and saw that it was surrounded by nothing but trees. The location was terrible and from what I could see, there were no other roads or entrances leading to the diner. It seemed that the only way to the diner was through the path by which I came.

After a couple of minutes, I heard the door opening. I hopped up and greeted a younger man standing in the doorway.

"Sir, please. I just need to use your phone. I have money. I only have to make one phone call."

"Your money is no good here. Come in. Please," the man said with a smile on his face as he gestured with his hand, inviting me into the building. "What's your name, if you don't mind me asking?"

I went to shake his hand. "George."

From first look, the plastic gloves and white apron helped me assume that he was a waiter or chef. The Middle Eastern man looked to be in his mid-30s and was medium in stature. His hair was short and curly, while his beard was unkempt and rough.

"Nice to meet you, George. My name is—"

"Emmanuel," I interrupted. "It's on your name tag."

"Well, lovely to meet you, George. Being that I have a name tag and flare all over my chest, you seem to know me better than I know you." Emmanuel chuckled at himself. "What are you doing out here in the middle of the forest anyway?"

"I apologize. I'm sorry about this whole thing. Did you hear anything about the earthquake back on the East Coast?"

"Earthquake?" he said surprised. "No, I didn't hear anything. It could be what caused that big mudslide back on the main highway. I did feel something earlier, could have been the tremor. Must have been a severe earthquake."

"The news is saying that it's the largest to ever hit the States. I've been trying to get back home to find my wife and daughter. I haven't been able to contact them since the earthquake hit. I've been driving and lost for hours. I ended up crashing my car just outside the forest."

"Wow. Are you okay?" Emmanuel asked shockingly.

"Yes, but could I please just use your phone? I really need to make a call. I promise I won't take too long."

"No problem, George. Go ahead and take a seat at that table, and I'll get that phone for you," Emmanuel said while pointing to a booth with red seat cushions and a white tabletop near the front window. "Do you need anything? Anything to eat or drink?"

"No, I'm fine; I don't plan to stay that long. I just have to make a quick phone call."

"Okay. I'll be right back."

"Oh wait!" I yelled. Emmanuel turned around before walking into the back room.

"Do you have a radio?"

Emmanuel smiled. "There's one in the back. I'll get that along with the phone."

"Thanks," I said before taking a seat and watching Emmanuel as he left through the doors.

I sat thinking about Carol and Mindy while I admired the comfortable feel of the diner. It had the classic black and white checkered floor tiles. The bar had red leather stools that matched the booths. The diner also had a nicely cleaned white counter with a chrome base. Nonetheless, I just couldn't understand why someone would place what looked to be a top-notch diner in the middle of the forest.

Three
THE CUP

You must first empty your cup of what is old and sour before you can fill it with what is good and new.

The back doors swung open, and Emmanuel dodged between them before they closed behind him. "Whew! Did you see that, George?" he asked, smiling and clutching an old radio and rotary phone between his arms with the cords dangling to the floor.

"All right, so here is the phone and here is the radio," he said, placing them on the table in front of me. "The radio needs a plug, and the phone needs a jack. I apologize if we're a little old school," he said smiling.

"Come here. Take the phone." Emmanuel picked up the radio and went over to the bar. He moved two of the bar stools apart and uncovered the plug socket within the bar's wall.

"What about the phone jack?" I asked, holding the old phone and looking around for a place to plug it in.

"We have only one, but we haven't used it in a while. It may not work. I don't think we kept up with the payments. It's on the other side of the bar. Go over there and you should see it on the right of the coffee machine," Emmanuel said while hunched over, trying to plug in the radio.

Behind the bar, I found the rusted phone jack, plugged in the cord, placed the phone on the counter and picked it up to listen for a dial tone. "Doesn't work."

"What was that, George?" Emmanuel asked, turning the radio static down.

"The phone doesn't work. You sure you don't have another jack?"

"Nope, that's the only one. Try cleaning the cord."

"Well, do you have another phone cord at least?"

"No cord either. I guess it's just not a pleasant day for you, George. I think I'm getting something with this radio. Should be working in a second."

"Who has only one phone and phone jack?" I muttered.

"What was that, George?" Emmanuel asked.

"Nothing, just still trying to get the phone to work."

"Got it!" Emmanuel said. "Come here. I'm getting something on the radio."

I dropped the phone cord, rushed over to the bar and put my ear to the radio.

"Right— here," Emmanuel said as he turned the station and got a signal strong enough that we could hear a static voice.

Traffic is still backed up, and the road won't be back open until around 7:00 in the morning. We've gotten reports that the Earthquake was felt throughout the entire U.S., and we believe it may have caused a massive mudslide here locally. The effects of—

"What happened?" I said as the radio faded to static.

"I have no idea. It's an old radio." Emmanuel turned the radio channel looking for a better signal, but nothing was coming in clear enough to hear. "Did you get the phone to work?" he asked.

"No. Are you sure you don't have another phone?"

"That was it. We don't use the phone. You're the first person that has ever come here asking for one."

I looked at Emmanuel confused. "You don't have customers needing to call in? What about for emergencies?"

Emmanuel shrugged. "I guess we haven't thought about that."

"How does someone make a reservation then?"

"Maybe we should look into getting a working phone. How does that sound?"

"It won't help now," I grumbled and tossed the phone cord on top of the bar. Bothered by Emmanuel's lack of urgency, I asked, "Do you at least have a car?"

"Yes! We have a truck. Hold on for a second. The keys are here somewhere."

Emmanuel opened and searched the drawers under the back counter. "Here it is!" he threw the key over the bar. "Go ahead and check it out. It's around back."

I anxiously bolted toward the front door before

Emmanuel stopped me, "Do you want me to come?"

"No, I'll be fine. I'll be sure to come back once I get things squared away. I certainly do appreciate your help."

"No problem. You're welcome, George," he said, still searching for a radio channel.

I ran outside and was to the side of the diner before I heard the door slam shut. Behind the diner stood an open wooden shed housing an old blue truck. I ran to the truck and used the key to open the rusted door. My heart pounded eagerly as I envisioned myself getting back home to Carol and Mindy.

I inserted the key into the ignition and turned: nothing. No roaring engine, no lights, no clicking sounds even. I turned the key again and got the same result. I thought that maybe I wasn't turning it hard enough, so I took the key out of the ignition, inserted it back in slowly and then carefully turned it with force: nothing still.

I tried turning on the lights only to realize that they weren't working either. I stepped out of the truck and pulled the handle to open the hood. After walking to the front and yanking the hood open, I was able to see the source of the problem. There was no engine, just empty space where it should have been.

My heart sank as I looked around the truck to see if I could find the engine lying around, but there was nothing. No engine in sight. I stopped searching after I realized that even if I were to find the engine, I had no way to put it back in the truck without the proper equipment, and from the looks of things, that wasn't going to happen because there were no tools lying around.

I sat on the front bumper of the truck and thought of Carol and Mindy being stuck in the earthquake. Staring down at the cracked cement of the shed, I knew it was over. Any hope that I had to get back home had vanished.

I got up and started to walk toward the front of the diner, but stopped to look around. Even if I were to have gotten it started, there wasn't a road to drive the truck down. That was when I knew that Emmanuel had to have known the truck didn't have an engine and that it didn't work.

I was angry when I arrived at the front door of the diner. When I tried to pull the door open, I found that I had been locked out. Looking through the glass door and windows, I was able to see that Emmanuel was gone and no one was in the diner. Taking a closer look, I also noticed that the radio and phone were gone.

I knocked on the door and after a few seconds, the elderly man who had first answered the door when I arrived stepped out from the swinging back doors and spotted me waving. He proceeded to walk toward my direction while grabbing his notebook and pen.

He slowly opened the door. "Do you have a reservation?"

"Reservation? How? For what?" I asked angrily. "I just left. I was just out back in the shed. Emmanuel told—"

"You know Emmanuel?" the man interrupted with a puzzled look.

"Yes. I was just—"

"Hold on for a moment. Let me ask him if he

knows you." The man pointed to the bench outside next to the door. He closed and locked the door before heading to the back.

As I waited out front of the diner, sitting on the bench, I thought about how odd Emmanuel and the elderly man were. I was still a bit baffled about the diner being in the middle of the woods. Not only that, but they had no working phone or radio, and now the old man was losing his memory.

I kept looking back through the diner's windows at the double doors to see if I could spot Emmanuel coming. After a few minutes, the old man returned to the door and opened it.

I stepped one foot into the doorway before he stopped me and placed his hand on my shoulder. "If you know Emmanuel, then why did you leave him?"

"I only went to the shed out back. I would have come back had I left. I just needed to borrow the truck."

The man smirked and slightly nodded his head. "Then the process must begin again. You haven't understood the price." He released my shoulder and pointed me to sit at the booth near the front window.

The man continued through the back doors, and a few minutes later Emmanuel came back out with water and a cup of cappuccino.

"Hey, George! Good to see you back," he said while walking to the table. He placed the cappuccino in front of me and then gave himself the cup of water. "What can I help you with?"

"Here's your key," I said, sliding the key to the truck across the table. "The truck doesn't have an engine, but I'm sure you knew that."

"Yes, I knew that," Emmanuel said

unapologetically.

"Was I just supposed to push the truck all the way back to Virginia?"

"Well. I'm sorry you are upset, George. You only asked me if I had a vehicle. You never mentioned you needed it to work."

"I didn't know I needed to be specific. Why would I ask you for a non-working truck?"

"Why are you upset? I only gave you what you asked for. Am I wrong for that? Maybe you should be upset with your expectation, not with me."

"I'm not going to worry about it. It's not your fault. I can't expect you to help me and then be upset when you don't," I said before turning to stare out the window.

After a few minutes of silence, Emmanuel asked, "George, I don't mean to offend you in any way, but have you tried to pray about it? Going to God never hurts."

"God? Go to him for what? Isn't he the cause of all of this?"

"How so?" Emmanuel asked with a raised eyebrow, before sitting back in his seat and crossing his arms.

"I know you may have your opinions, Emmanuel, but in a nutshell, God is cruel. I know you might think that he doesn't command the disasters that occur on earth, but he does. While he may not make them happen, he does give them permission to happen. If it weren't for him, my wife and daughter would be safe right now instead of—" I stopped myself as I considered the devastating condition they might be in, and I didn't want to hear myself say what I was about say.

"What do you mean he approves it?" Emmanuel questioned.

"He allows it to happen. He is supposed to know everything. He could have stopped this earthquake. If we are all just going to die, then let us die peacefully. He only placed us here on Earth so that he could see us all suffer and then run to him. What kind of God is that? If this is what he wanted, then he should have just killed us all off a long time ago. There was no need to make mankind. For what? For this? Cruel, that's your God."

"I can understand your pain, and I see your point, George. Now let me ask you, why did you decide to have a child?"

"What does that have to do with anything?"

"Just answer the question. It has a lot to do with how you view God. Why is it that you decided to have a child?"

"I don't know. I had my reasons, and my wife had hers. We just decided that it was time and nothing was holding us back. What does it matter?"

"I want you to understand something. Now, think about it. What did you gain or would you have gained by having a child? What in your heart made you desire a child? You say the timing was right, but right for what? Why did you decide to bring a child into this world?"

Emmanuel placed his hands on the table and leaned forward waiting for my answer.

I looked up to the ceiling, calmed my anger and thought about what Emmanuel had asked. When the answer came to mind, I figured out where he was going with the question. I looked back at him and saw him smiling.

"You get it now, don't you, George?" He asked before relaxing in his seat. "God doesn't want anyone to suffer. He just wants you to have a chance because he loves you. Just as you wanted and still want for your daughter. You wanted to share your life and your success. That is the real reason you had a child. You seem to be a knowledgeable man, so you know that the world isn't a perfect place. However, you still brought your daughter into this imperfect world to give her a chance to be successful. You would give her anything she asks, but you know she would still need to choose her own path. In return, you ask only that she loves you. That is how God is. He only wanted to share himself. He desired us to have an opportunity. All that he asks in return is for us to love him. Would you be a better father or man if you chose to never bring your daughter into this corrupt world? Should you just take the life of everyone you love, simply because you don't want to see them suffer throughout their journey in life? Do you get it now, George?"

I answered, not wanting to show Emmanuel any sign of giving in to his theory. "I doubt that. God isn't that simple."

"That's where you are confused, George. God *is* that simple. Love is surprisingly easy. If anything, it's harder not to love than it is to love. I know that's something you understand particularly well."

Emmanuel leaned in closer. "God loves you even more than you love your family, and you're here in this world because of his love."

"If I just love God, then that's it? I can just sit back in my house and watch TV until I'm dead and go to Heaven? That sounds too simple."

"Because it is. Loving is the most natural thing you can do. However, if you truly love someone, would you want to sit around and do nothing, knowing that they desire something from you? Could you truly call that love?"

I replied. "So you're saying that in order to love, I must do something about it?"

"Exactly!" Emmanuel said, snapping his fingers. "I knew you were smart, George. In order to love God—or anyone for that matter—you can't just do nothing. To ignore their desires is to not love them. It's that simple."

I pondered for a moment before countering his statement. "Let's say I do understand and agree with what you're saying. But now the question is, if God loves me, then why doesn't he do as I desire?"

"That's simple also, George. He's God." Emmanuel nodded his head and raised his hand as if I had asked a rhetorical question.

"What is that supposed to mean?"

"It means that God is more important than you. To say that your desires are more valuable than his is to say that you are more important than him.

"If your wife and daughter both desired something out of you that required you to choose between the two of them, whom would you offer higher power and authority to?"

Emmanuel waited for my response. When he realized I wasn't going to voluntarily help him prove his point, he continued. "You would give priority and higher authority to your wife, or you should at least. Even though you may think you love them alike, your wife is the higher power, and as long as she is asking something of you that is reasonable, you must place her desires above your daughter's desires. God's desires must be placed above your wife's, children, family, friends, things and even self. He is the highest authority, and what he desires should extend above everything and everyone in your life."

"So what is it that God desires from us besides love?" I asked, becoming more interested in the conversation.

"The question isn't just what God desires. It's also what love desires."

"So, how did we get to love? What about God?"

"God is love and love is God. The God part of God desires a relationship, but the love part of him desires an action."

Emmanuel looked at me and saw my confusion. "Love is in doing, and God is in believing, and God is Love. You cannot love doing for God and not love God. In the same manner, you cannot love God and not love doing for God. They are one-in-the-same."

Once Emmanuel realized I wasn't catching on, he continued by answering my original question. "Love desires that you share and spread it. Tell everyone you know about love so that the world can know. If you spread the word, that defines the love of God, then the world may know of God."

"Okay, I understand it now," I said, partially grasping the concept. "That sounds simple."

"It is, George."

Emmanuel reflected for a moment before he took my empty cup of cappuccino and looked inside to make sure that it wasn't full before placing it back on the table. He then swiped the cup off the table, and it shattered into pieces on the floor.

I jumped back surprised and looked at him wide-eyed.

"Man is like this broken cup," he said calmly. "A broken cup cannot support what God wants to share with it. You must fix your cup so that you can preserve and grasp all that God desires to give you."

Emmanuel got down on the floor and started to pick up the pieces. He placed them on the table one by one. "Everyone is broken, George," he said as he stared at one of the pieces. "No cup ever wants to remain broken; it tries to avoid and ignore the fact. God will pour himself into it, but it will always drain. It may search and find small pieces of itself here and there, but ultimately, every cup wants to be made whole and placed within the china cabinet."

I sat back comfortably in my seat. "So, if we are all broken and no one can enter this 'china cabinet,' then what is the purpose of it all? None of us will ever be good enough for God. To say that I am broken is to say that he made a broken person and, from my understanding, God can't create anything imperfect."

"That's where you are mistaken, George. God created man to be good and perfect. However, you are seeing the effects of his original creation. For example, if someone gave you a perfect apple and you then destroyed it, is that apple still perfect? "

"I assume it wouldn't be, as it's destroyed."

"Right, so who do you blame for the destroyed apple? Do you blame the person who gave you the perfect apple, or do you blame yourself for destroying the apple? It's not God who is cruel. Man is the cruel one, George."

Emmanuel finished cleaning up the cup and sat back in his seat.

I thought for a moment before continuing. "I think I might be able to get you a job with the firm I work for. You seem to know a lot about this. We could really use you if you're interested. I'm sure you'd make more money with us than you are making here."

Emmanuel fell back in his seat laughing. "Thanks for the offer, but I'll have to pass on the opportunity for now."

I tried to avoid that he was laughing at my proposition, so I continued back on topic. "If we're broken, then that's it? Adam and Eve just broke all of us from perfection? It still helps prove my point that no one is perfect any longer. Everyone is still broken."

Emmanuel continued to chuckle at my job offer before taking a drink of water and answering, "That is true. However, God didn't just leave you or me here without giving us a chance. He sent us super glue.

"Jesus is the glue to fix the broken cups. Without it, the cups can't be fixed. You must fix your cup, so that God can pour into it. Jesus is the only glue strong enough to hold the cups together. Without him, the cups will never be truly fixed."

"What about another type of glue? What about Muhammad glue or Buddha glue? Why is it that Jesus is the only glue in your opinion that can fix this broken cup?"

Emmanuel smiled and answered, "People will always have their personal beliefs, and they are allowed that. Nonetheless, my belief is that Jesus was and is the only glue given by the Potter himself. Trust the glue that was given by the manufacturer. It's the only one that has a warranty." Emmanuel chuckled with his response.

"Let's just say that I do believe in what you're saying, but why does God not just give us a new cup instead of trying to glue the old one back together?"

"He doesn't do this because he knows the cup can be fixed. Each cup is special to him and has a personal place within his heart *or* china cabinet. To replace the cup is to say that the cup is worthless and beyond repair. God believes that every cup can be repaired. He loves each cup no matter how strong or damaged it is. If someone you love were broken mentally or physically, would you not love them still as they are?"

"I assume I would," I answered as I considered Carol, Mindy and my other family and friends. Surprising, I knew Emmanuel was right. Even if broken, I would still care for the ones I love as they are.

"Come here, George," Emmanuel said while getting up and going behind the bar.

As we approached the shining chrome and black cappuccino maker, Emmanuel checked to make sure it was plugged in. "I know you may think that life is difficult, but it's fairly easy."

He grabbed a coffee mug that was already half-filled with old, dark wine and moved it next to the cappuccino maker.

"It's just like a cappuccino really. There are many ingredients, all to get one result. The cup itself is like the vessel of man. It is what holds the gift of God."

I stood and watched as he poured cold, clear water into the machine's chamber and secured the boiler cap.

"The water is like the spirit. It fills the body to

sustain life."

He started to grind the coffee beans before placing the grounds into the filter and tamping them. "The beans are the essence of life. They are used to create, grow and transform."

After brushing off the excess grounds, he placed the filter into the machine.

"The coffee maker is like the Son of God. It transforms the beans into something new."

He then took the half-full cup of old wine, placed it under the spout and turned on the machine.

He poured milk into an additional metal cup and frothed it, making it thick and creamy.

"The milk is like love. It's the topping used to complete the perfect cappuccino."

As the cappuccino started to pour from the spout, it fell into the old wine and mixed until the glass was full. Emmanuel took the cream, blended it over the espresso and finished it by creating a heart-shaped design within the cappuccino.

"See this, George," he said, picking up the steaming cappuccino and holding it up to me with a smile. "The perfect cappuccino."

He handed me the warm mug and watched, waiting for me to take a sip. Knowing that I had no intention to drink the mixture, I responded. "There was already something in this cup. I think it was wine."

Emmanuel's smile widened, and he took the cup from my hands and poured the drink into the sink. He looked back at me and said softly, "You must first empty your cup of what is old and sour before you can fill it with what is good and new."

I chuckled before pondering on all that

Emmanuel had taught me in such a short conversation. I stood gazing at him, watching him clean up, before my attention turned to the clock—*1:17a.m.*

"I need to go!" I exclaimed. "Thank you so much for the talk, Emmanuel, but I have to get to my wife." I ran from behind the bar and went to the front door of the diner.

Arriving at the door, I grabbed the door-knob and stepped one foot out before a powerful explosion of wind picked me up and hurled me back into the diner, slamming me against a bar stool and knocking me unconscious.

Four
THE BEANS

Why do you turn your back on God because of what man has done?

I awoke hours later to a slightly troubled look on Emmanuel's face. He held a warm cloth against my forehead.

"What was that?" I yelled, jumping out of the seat I had been comfortably reclined in. "Was it another earthquake?"

Emmanuel and the old man stared, watching me as I frantically looked around the diner and out the window in search of storm damage. "Where's the radio? Did you feel that? Are you two okay?"

Turning to the old man, without saying anything, Emmanuel nodded his head and the old man took the warm cloth and hot water before he left through the back doors of the diner.

"I need to get back to my wife!" I exclaimed, sprinting toward the door.

Emmanuel stood in my way. "George, please

calm down. You will never find your way without me. You'll only get lost out there."

"Well, let's go then," I said, nudging my way pass Emmanuel.

"I will show you, but can I first ask something of you?" Emmanuel asked as he stood behind me with his hand on my shoulder.

I turned and faced him. "What? What do you need?"

"Just stay and talk with me a little while longer," Emmanuel said kindly. "You don't understand how much it would mean to me. I really enjoy your conversations. I haven't asked you for much of anything."

I stood with one hand on the glass door looking out at the forest. From behind the distant mountains, the early sunlight lit the pine trees. Somehow, the morning light showered me with peace. Calmed, I stood gazing out the window fascinated by how the sun had taken the once eerie forest and turned it into an alluring composition of beauty. Watching in admiration, I could almost smell the glittering spring flowers adorning the entrance back into the wooded area.

Being drawn into the enticement of the forest, I started to push open the door. "George, you'll be out there for hours," Emmanuel interrupted my trance. "Following me will make the journey much easier. I know the way. Trust me."

I don't know why, but somehow I knew Emmanuel was right about him making the journey easier. Because the restaurant stood in the middle of the woods, I figured he might have been through the forest a few times, enough to know his way at least.

I pulled myself away from the door and turned to face him. "Okay, but I don't have long."

A smile formed on Emmanuel's face, and he directed me to take a seat at the booth next to the door.

We both sat without saying anything. I stared out the window, and when I would occasionally glance at Emmanuel from the corner of my eye, I could see him staring at me and grinning as if I were a lover whom he admired.

To resolve the awkwardness and silence, I started the conversation. "What do you want to talk about?"

"We can talk about anything!" Emmanuel said enthusiastically. "You haven't told me much about yourself or your family actually. All I understand is that you are married with a daughter. You never told me anything about where you are coming from either."

I hadn't thought about it before then, but as Emmanuel spoke, I realized he had no clue who I was. Here I was, some practically deranged man running into the diner after appearing out of the woods.

"I'm sorry about all of this, Emmanuel. I didn't even think about you. Did you really not hear anything about the earthquake?"

"I think we felt a small shock, but that was all. How did you end up here because of an earthquake?"

I took a deep breath, sat back in my seat, and told him everything about the business meeting, the car accident, the earthquake, and almost being crushed by a tree in the forest before finding the diner.

After I finished, Emmanuel continued. "Well, you must be starving. Hold on; let us get you something to eat."

The old man came from behind the back doors almost as if he had been waiting for his cue.

When he arrived at the table, Emmanuel asked me, "Are you okay with a bagel, eggs, sausage and a cup of coffee?"

Just as I was about to decline his offer, my stomach roaring validated how hungry I was. The sounds startled Emmanuel, and he smiled when he saw the embarrassment on my face. He nodded his head to the old man, who then left to prepare the meal.

"Who is he?" I whispered after the old man left through the back doors.

Emmanuel whispered back. "Who is who?" he asked with a confused look.

"The old man who was just here."

Emmanuel laughed. "Old man? Don't let him hear you say that. That's Cephas—or should I say, 'old man' Cephas."

"So is he the chef or the door man?"

"Cephas is neither." Emmanuel continued to laugh. "He's a good friend of mine. We've been together for a long time. I really do love Cephas." Emmanuel smiled before going into thought. "Now tell me about your family," he said, smacking my hand that had been resting on the table.

I pulled back and rested comfortably in the seat. "Well, I've been married for almost 8 years now. My wife's name is Carol. My daughter's name is Mindy and she's five years old."

"How did you and your wife meet?"

"That's actually a long story. I only wish I had the time to tell you all about it. Not only that, but I really don't want to think about my family right now. Please, ask another question."

"I understand," Emmanuel replied. "Tell me about your work then. You said you're out here because of it. Being that you offered me a job, I assume it has something to do with religion."

I knew that by telling Emmanuel what I did, it would begin a long conversation that I would probably lose.

"Yes, I work in religion. I help market churches," I said, hoping to get by with the brief explanation.

"Market churches? What do you mean market churches?"

"Just that: market churches. I'm sure you market your diner. Just as you market *it*, I help churches with their marketing campaigns."

Emmanuel shrugged his shoulders. "I think I understand."

"It's not that the company I work for is called, 'church marketing company.' I work in marketing, but I'm particularly good at marketing churches, so that's what I do."

"How did that happen? How did you get involved in marketing for churches? Did you just wake up one morning and the idea hit you that you wanted to do that for a living?"

"I wouldn't say that. However, it was a pretty random decision. At the time, I was in college working on my degree in marketing. I decided to just put my skills to use one day to help a church member's family. The woman's husband and a deacon of the church died, and I helped put together the plans to raise money for the funeral and home expenses. After I did a good job and because I enjoyed it, I was asked to manage all of the marketing and promotional needs for my church's events. That was how it began. However, I now work for a marketing firm that specializes in ministry marketing."

Emmanuel nodded his head. "That was great what you did. It's always good to love what you do."

"Yeah—I should."

"What's wrong? You don't like marketing?"

"I can't say that I do. I used to. I used to love it a lot. Now it's just what I do, not what I love."

"What happened? Why the loss of interest?"

"I had a reality check. Matter-of-fact, I can't even remember the last time I actually went to church without Carol practically forcing me. Somewhere along the path, I just got tired. Tired of the same thing, the lies, stories, drama, just everything about religion."

Emmanuel frowned. "That doesn't sound good. Can you explain a little better? Did you have a random thought that stopped you from believing, or was it a personal experience of some sort?"

After I recalled the occurrence, I answered Emmanuel's question. "It started at an event I attended at a mega-church that hired me for my services. When churches hire me, I sometimes first visit to get an idea of what they are like as a people and how they operate.

"In order to create a successful solution, I have to first find the problems. Going to the church allows me to see exactly what I'm working with. Once I find those problems, I develop solutions for them and incorporate those ideas into the marketing plan. My strategies generally consist of rebranding the image of the church. That involves looking at the logo, the catch phrase, the colors; building or redesigning the website; researching the neighboring competitors, et cetera. In a nutshell, my job is to make the church look more important than it is. Nevertheless, the main things I watched for were the leaders and members. I would learn the people and then add to my marketing plan ways in which that particular type of people needed to be addressed and motivated in order to produce positive results.

"Nonetheless, while attending that event several years ago, an older man sat next to me in the congregation. The first thing I noticed about him was that he didn't smell good. Based on his unkempt wardrobe and bad hygiene, I labeled him as possibly being homeless.

"The church was crowded because of the event and, unfortunately, there was nowhere else for him or me to sit. He arrived late, and the church was practically filled to capacity; one of the only remaining seats was right next to me. After getting the first whiff of his odor, I remember turning toward him and being greeted by a nearly flawless smile. As he shook my hand, he stretched over to my ear and introduced himself. I will never forget his name: Moses.

"Throughout the event, the man never spoke a word and only nodded his head often, smiled when he agreed and looked to me as his partner when the Bishop often told the members to look to their neighbor.

"As the event was nearing the end, it was time to give an offering. People reached into their pockets to get out their wallets. From the corner of my eye, I noticed Moses rifling through his pockets for change. When he finished, he had pulled out three pennies and clinched them in his fist. He continued to look around at everyone else, and I felt that perhaps he was ashamed of his giving. My natural thought was that maybe he should be ashamed of that small amount. It would have been better if he just hadn't pulled out any money at all.

Nonetheless, when it was time to stand, he also stood and repeated the words of the Bishop with everyone else who prayed over the tithe and offering.

"As the Bishop finished praying, he first asked if there were any members who could give $1,000. As almost 20 people stood, he then asked if anyone could give $500 and then $100. All of those who were able to offer the higher amounts between $100 and $500 were asked to come down to the stage. After they added their gifts to the bucket, they returned to their seats. Then the Bishop continued by asking those who could give $1,000 to come down to the stage. As many people went down, they all stood in a line, being acknowledged and giving their testimonies one after the other. As each man and woman spoke, I could see Moses clinch his fist harder and tighter. By the time the microphone had reached the fourth person within the long line of givers, Moses threw down his coins, grabbed his jacket and shoved his way through the aisle before exiting through the back doors.

"I thought to follow him, but I was somewhat clouded as to why he left. However, the more I thought about it, I realized that somehow he took offense by not being able to give. When I saw others giving $1,000, I remember thinking that they must have been blessed and that I would love to be as fortunate, with the ability to give back to the Church.

“It was only once I arrived at my hotel that night that I understood why Moses was upset. The answer I came up with was that somehow the church that night had created a ranking system based on the givers’ amount. I guess the problem was, why did Moses’ three pennies not afford him the opportunity to give his testimony and meet the popular Bishop at the front. I'm sure he had a better testimony than any of us at the event. Somehow, he felt judged, and I hadn’t realized it, but that was exactly what happened. I had even judged him as being homeless simply based on how he looked. I had placed myself above him. I hadn’t even noticed that the Bishop had done the same.

“While I looked at those givers as generous men and women who wanted to contribute to the congregation and ultimately help spread the Gospel, Moses made me realize that maybe the church had gone about it the wrong way by publicly presenting the finances of others. He made me rethink what I was doing as a church marketer who focused mainly on making the Church money.

“I understood then that being blessed wasn't about how much you possessed or were able to give. As a strategy to obtain financial support for churches, I would place techniques within my marketing pitches that would help churches find appropriate ways to ask the members for more money. Some involved ways of simply asking. Others involved using scripture to encourage. Another involved using scripture to shame. Each strategy was selected depending on the type of audience within that church. The end result was that the church would profit more financially.

“However, even with all of that, I never really

thought about the members beyond anything more than a number. How many and how much was all I ever cared to know.

"That night after meeting Moses, I realized he felt just as I saw him—as a number. He was only three pennies worth. The reality was that if he had walked down to the front of the church offering three pennies and looking the way he did, the Bishop's security team would have seized him. Giving a testimony would have been out of the question.

"That night I came up with a great new marketing strategy for that church to gain new members like Moses. I still remember the name of the flyer and titles I suggested using: *'To believe is not enough.'*

"When I presented the 43-page plan to the church leaders, they ended up telling me that they didn't want low-income members; they wanted to focus on the higher-end suburb area of the community to gain better financial support.

"From that moment, it started happening more and more with other churches. I quickly got lost in it all again. I would simply change my plans to focus on finances, and every church was pleased with the results.

"I remember once I even got mad at having met Moses. I didn't like the way he made me rethink everything I knew. I felt he was ruining my career.

"Nonetheless, the more I learned the details of how each church operates, the further I got away from the meaning of it. I just didn't see the love of the people causing the movements within them. The Church was more interested in its members' activities, finances and building blueprints than they were in focusing on the words of the Bible. I found myself no longer wanting to grow with the Church, but I wanted to grow out of it. If the Church is supposed to be like Jesus in Heaven, then I have no desire to follow that polluted religion or the God that it belongs to."

"So are you saying that you aren't a follower of Christ any longer?" Emmanuel asked, showing interest in the conversation.

"I don't think I was ever a real follower to begin with."

"How so?"

"I can't say that I ever really believed. I don't accept that I can say I loved you yesterday, but not today. If you love, then you always love. I assume believing is or should be the same concept. Maybe I was just a part of an organization or movement and didn't really know it. I had become a fan of my religion, attracted to the events and people. However, I can't really say that I was a real Christ-follower. I was more of a people- or church-follower than I was a Christ-follower. I went to church to please my wife or to make someone else happy. It never gratified me in any manner. I didn't go to church and feel the warmth of God. I never prayed and felt the spirit come over me or fell in love with reading or hearing the word of God.

"My company helps churches market. Almost every time that I would ask a church what they wanted to improve on, they would say finances or building a new church to gain recognition of success. I realized then that churches didn't care about getting the souls of the member's right. It was only secondary, or an afterthought. Their priorities focused mainly on gaining income. I hated those meetings with church leaders. They would judge me as soon as

I walked through the door to greet them. If I didn't shake hands properly or stand a certain way, even if I didn't shave cleanly enough, I would have to hear their complaints. Church leaders are some of the biggest judgers I know: politics, relationships, fashion, money, gossip, sex and gender, even down to what I could eat and say. It's not that I don't want to go to and grow with a church, it's just that the Church creates too many of its own rules, personalized from whichever particular group of scriptures they choose from the various translations of the Bible."

"If you know so much and know what is wrong with the Church, then why not fix it?" Emmanuel interrupted. "Why not call them out on their mistakes? It sounds like you know exactly what you need to do. You've found your problem and solution, so what are you waiting for?"

"That's just the thing, Emmanuel. I don't care to fix it. I simply no longer care about the system. It's what I do to make a living. The only thing I care about is stability and survival. If there really is a God, then he can fix it himself."

Emmanuel nodded. "Interesting outlook."

Surprised by Emmanuel's lack of response, I asked, "That's all you have to say? I expected you to have more of an opinion."

"I can say a lot, but do you really want to hear what I have to say? You seem to already have your mind made up. It sounds like you've been thinking and creating your opinion for years."

"You'd be correct in thinking that. It comes from years of studying and observing the religion. I'm not just some unbeliever who knows nothing about the religion. I know everything I need to know. I've seen everything I needed to see, and I've heard everything I needed to hear. The whole thing is just a game that I have no desire to play."

Emmanuel and I sat in silence for a moment before I continued. "Actually, I am interested in what you have to say."

Emmanuel leaned in and placed his elbows on the table. "You aren't wrong in your thinking, George, but I do believe you are judging the wrong thing.

"You're not upset with the Church at all—you're upset with man. You're upset because man has disappointed you, not the Church. In addition, you shouldn't allow yourself to use the Church as a crutch for your walk with God. You're seeking a temple or an example figure to follow, but what you do not understand is that there is only one direction to follow, and that is the direction of Jesus. He is the example. If you ever follow man, you will always be disappointed. Why do you turn your back on God or Jesus because of what man has done?"

"Because God allows it," I said confidently.

"God allows all, George, but you allow yourself also. He allows opportunity. It's up to you to follow the appropriate ones. Having options and opportunity is only as damaging as you allow it to be. Do you blame your parents for all of your mistakes because they gave you an opportunity to make them?"

Emmanuel paused. "Of course you don't. Just because someone gives freedom, doesn't mean that the person who receives it will do right with it.

"You can't continue on this path, George. You can't betray God for financial security or personal pleasures. Yes, some churches have and do continue to use the name of Jesus for their own agendas.

However, it is your responsibility to find the correct path. The Church or religion—whether good or bad—isn't going to get you in or out of Heaven. To truly follow Jesus you must abandon yourself and others. Jesus never told you to follow anyone but him.

"You have mistaken what church really is. A church is a gathering of two or more people who fellowship about Jesus and the Father. What you and I are doing here now is considered church."

Emmanuel and I both sat quietly for a moment before he continued. "Are you perfect, George?"

"Of course not," I answered.

"Well, there you have it. You and I together have created an imperfect church. A church of flaws, sin and mistakes. The Church isn't perfect—it's human. Church is filled with saved sinners. To say that a human doesn't sin, is to say that humans are perfect, which is far from the truth.

"Being a true Christ-follower isn't about going to a building, being sinless, performing rituals, paying tithes, what you wear, your education or doing good deeds. It's not at all about how others perceive you. It's not about your position at church, your denomination, your relationships with others or your status at work or within politics. It's whether you have accepted Jesus into your heart and as your personal Savior. That is it.

"It is the obligation of the Church to build up and equip with knowledge so that they can expand upon Jesus' teachings to the world. The local church is to be a place of fellowship, prayer and devotion with one another as a family. Ultimately, it should be a place of training up believers and preparing them to proclaim the Gospel.

"No man is the head of the Church. No pastor, pope, preacher or elder. Jesus is and should be the Church's authority. There is no unity more important than Jesus' message and a relationship with him. Jesus is the head, the body and the heart of the Church. If he builds the Church, then no one and no thing can overcome it.

"Jesus is not concerned with you knowing Bible verses or praying a certain way, walking down an aisle or repeating certain verses of the Bible after your church leaders. That doesn't concern him. These people honor Jesus with their lips, but their hearts are far from him. These things are unacceptable and are not what produce a true and faithful follower. A follower is someone who has undoubtedly received Jesus as his Savior and follows him as best as he humanly can as the seed of the Gospel penetrates his heart's soil."

"I don't know if I'm ready to accept Jesus into my heart just yet," I said emotionally, as by now I knew Emmanuel could see the internal struggle I was having with my spirituality.

He continued, "Is Jesus so unworthy that you must *accept* him? Should he not be the one accepting you? You don't accept a reward—you yearn for it. Does a drunkard accept alcohol? Does a gambler accept winnings? Jesus is the prize. He is the reward. If you want it, it will be given to you. You cannot buy his love or manipulate your way into his heart."

Emmanuel paused and thought. "Where your treasure is, there your heart will be also. Let Jesus be your treasure, George. If he doesn't have you fully, then you don't have him at all. You can't compare him. You can't want what he has to offer and not desire to put in the work to attain it. God and his Son are real, George. They aren't some comfort products that you can buy and sell."

I stopped trying to hold back the tears that were drowning my eyes. "How am I supposed to get to Heaven if God only allows perfect people there? I'm far from perfect. I've tried and if I haven't gotten faith, love and a fellowship by now, then I'll never get it."

Emmanuel placed his hand on my head that was now faced down between my arms on the table. "George, we all have sinned, we all will sin. By believing in Jesus, you aren't required to become a sinless person. You are to become a person who tries through all of the troubles and difficulties.

"Human perfection doesn't exist. Trying is all that is asked of you. With God, with Jesus and with the power of the Holy Spirit, trying should come a little easier each day that you try with them. The issue here isn't whether you are capable; it is whether you understand the true power and capabilities within yourself. To try is to be successful. You only fail if you stop trying. That is all that God asks of you. Try it his way. When it doesn't work, keep trying. While success may be limited, trying is a guaranteed way to show God that you are willing and worthy to be in his Kingdom.

"God loves everyone the same. He is a God of love. He *is* love. However, he especially loves those who love him. Moreover, by loving Jesus, you find mercy and love from his Father. Loving Jesus is your attempt at trying to be closer to God.

"You are here for a reason, George. All of

humanity is. It is not a coincidence that the earth, stars, sun and moon just happened to have landed in the right spots. It is no accident that the heart beats; and the brain functions; and the water flows; and the eyes see; and the veins pump your blood in such a mechanism that one miscalculation would destroy your living being."

Emmanuel moved my arms and raised my head with his hand. Looking into my drenched eyes, he asked, "What if there really is a Heaven and Hell? What if God were real and life came down to the one question of whether you believe or not?

"If life is a game, then by playing it with Jesus you'll win every time. If he doesn't exist, then everyone wins. However, if he does exist, then many will lose. By following Jesus, you will always win the game of life and insure your soul. It should be an easy decision. The question you need to ask yourself is, what do you gain by not believing—and whatever you feel you do gain, is it worth the gamble of eternal damnation?"

I thought about what Emmanuel was asking until I looked over at the clock.

I got up from the table. "I think our time is done," I said, drying my eyes. "I'll definitely be back, Emmanuel. You're a good man."

Emmanuel stood up. "Is there any way I could persuade you to stay longer?"

"Not now. I really do have to go," I said, heading toward the door only to be interrupted by Emmanuel placing his hand on the glass.

"What are you doing?" I asked.

As I looked toward Emmanuel for an answer, my eyes were nearly blinded by a glare of sunlight beaming through an opening in his wrist.

I stood speechlessly staring at the hole. Outside dark clouds suddenly filled the sky with signs of an impending storm. Thunder struck and the ground trembled as I grabbed on to the nearest post.

"What's going on? Who are you?" I yelled, backing away.

Emmanuel took his hand from the door, came toward me and answered. "I am Who I am."

Five
THE MILK

Know me for who I am and not for who you want me to be.

"Take a seat, George." Emmanuel motioned his hand toward the nearest booth.

"No. What is this? I'm not sitting down until you tell me what's going on."

Emmanuel walked over to the table and sat down with his back toward me. "Please, sit down," he said, without turning around.

"You were scared, George. You felt weak and powerless. You reacted like a man in love. The life of your family was in danger, and you responded the only way you knew how. It's an easy decision for someone in love to give his life. I know you love Carol and Mindy, and I knew long ago that you would make that sacrifice for them. You're a good man, George."

I shouted and cried as my emotions overwhelmed me, remembering the frightful robbery. "What do you mean you were there? What do you think this is—a joke? You're wrong, you know that? You shouldn't play with people like this. Innocent people died that night, and you're trying to capitalize on it for your own selfish gratifications. What are you getting out of this anyway? Why bring up that night? You have no idea what it's like to have someone you love be threatened like that."

I went to the door and slammed my fist against the glass. "You don't know anything about me!"

"I know you, George, and I knew you even before you were."

Emmanuel stood and walked toward me. "Your secrets are my own. Your desires are embedded within my spirit. Those who you love, I love more deeply. I have experienced every moment of your success and your failure. Before, during and after all of your thoughts and your doings, I am, was and will always be. Not only do I know your wife, Carol, I also love and adore her the same as you. Your daughter, Mindy." Emmanuel paused and smiled. "As creative and outspoken as she is, her life is more precious to me than anything of this world."

As he moved closer and placed his hand on my shoulder, I pushed him away and grabbed the door handle to leave.

A bolt of lightning struck the ground and the storm roared louder and heavier. I watched as ominous clouds began to cover the sky. I gazed out at the storm, trying to compose myself before turning around to face Emmanuel.

"Am I dead?" I asked timidly.

"If you take a seat, I'll tell you everything you need to know."

I waited for a few minutes before walking slowly

over to the red cushioned seat and sat down.

"Who are you?" I asked apprehensively, without giving eye contact, focusing my attention on a rip in the vinyl on the side of the table.

Emmanuel came over to the table and sat down across from me. "You know who I am."

"I don't know if I do," I said with my head down still. "Is your name really Emmanuel?"

"That is just one of my many names. However, what you call me isn't as important as how you view me."

Still tensed, I found myself uncontrollably glancing at Emmanuel's wrist, trying to find the marks I had seen earlier, but they somehow seemed to have vanished.

I watched silently in discomfort as Emmanuel gazed out the window before looking back at me. "It's time we define our relationship, George."

I looked up and glared into Emmanuel's luminous brown eyes. I hadn't noticed before, but he had the most piercingly beautiful and kind eyes that I had ever seen. Captivated by the glory of his presence, I became unguarded. I felt a peace that I hadn't felt in a long time. Even as I clearly knew who Emmanuel truly was, I continued to refute it as I probed for assurance.

"How? Why? You just can't be—him. You don't even look like him."

Emmanuel raised his eyebrows. "Have you ever seen *him* before? Do you only trust and believe me if I look a certain way? Should I have long hair and wear a white robe? Should I look like a traditional rabbi in order to obtain your trust?"

I tried to correct myself. "I'm not saying that you

should look a certain way. You just look so casual and…updated."

Emmanuel smiled and placed his elbows on the table. "I only look this way to help make you comfortable. Without this flesh, you would simply wither away at the sight of me, as I would be nothing more than a blaze of radiance."

After a moment of thought, I asked another question to see if I could catch Emmanuel in a lie. "I thought man was created in the image of God. Shouldn't you look like you do now? Like a man?"

"George, if you know anything about God, then you should know that no man can ever see God and live. God is made of Spirit. Man is created in *that* image of God. You are created in the spiritual likeness of God. It wouldn't make sense for God to have the same physical parts as you.

"If God were physical and you were created in his image, then that would suggest that your physical body would be everlasting as God is. However, that is not the case. Man is like God through his spirit self and not his physical self. The spirit you is infinite just as God is, and the physical you will at some point die.

"God has presented himself often as a physical man, but it was only so that man could find comfort in him."

"Shouldn't you be speaking in Hebrew or Aramaic?"

"I can speak in any language that I desire." Emanuel laughed. "I wouldn't be God at all if I had a language barrier."

While I tried to think of more questions, Emmanuel interrupted my thoughts.

"George, I know you have a lot of questions

about me. I expect you to. However, to help you answer most of them, you have to first understand that the only way for you to truly receive me is to stop expecting me. Know me for who I am and not for who you want me to be."

"Who do you think I want you to be?"

"Just a man," Emmanuel answered.

I dwelled on the thought and realized how correct he was. I had just figured him to be a man. Throughout most of my life, that was how I viewed him. In order to keep myself above him, I classified him as just being a meager man with faults and problems.

"Couldn't you have done something about it? About the shooting?" I asked earnestly. "There must have been something."

"Did you ask for something to be done?" Emmanuel asked, turning to look at me. "Blessings come through prayer, George. Sometimes it's that simple."

"Why do I or anyone have to ask or pray? I just don't get it. I just hate the way this whole thing works. Why won't you just be a blessing to everyone without attaching a stipulation to your supposed kindness?"

"To answer your question, yes, you should ask. What do you think is the right thing to do? You seem to have all of the answers. Knowing what you think you know about me, what do you believe I should have done?"

"Anything! It's just not right for innocent people to be murdered or tortured because of someone else's inability to cope with their inadequate life or lack of success."

Emmanuel replied, "If you understand that, then

you understand the sacrifice of what I went through.

“It's not that I don’t want to bless everyone; it's that most don't ask or desire to be blessed by me. Many don’t care to know me, and I won’t force my way into a heart until I’m invited in. Not just that, but I don't desire to control anyone’s choices. Doing that wouldn't be beneficial to the appreciation of the precious life that was gifted to all of man.”

"I’m not saying that, I understand. I get it. It just doesn't feel right. If I had all the power in the world and beyond, I just think I would use it for good, to protect everyone. I’m just saying that it feels like something more could have been done.”

“You’re a smart man, George. You seem to understand even when you don’t know you do. Yes, I do have the power to protect and save everyone. However, everyone can use my power if they simply ask. What is simpler than asking? Am I asking too much? I gave my life, and in return I ask only for adoration. That’s it. To sacrifice life for love sounds like a fair trade to me. Was my life not enough that you ask me for more without giving me anything?”

I turned my attention out the window and thought of what Emmanuel asked. Maybe I was thinking a bit selfishly. What can I compare the life of God to?

I continued. “Why am I here? What do you want from me anyway?”

“It’s not about what I want from you. I’m here because you called me.”

“I called you? I don’t remember ever praying to you. Not unless—,” I stopped myself as I thought of the few times I had prayed. It was usually only when in the presence of churchgoers while I was trying to sell them my marketing pitch. I hadn't actually prayed one-on-one to God in years. "When and why would I have called you?"

"Your spirit has called out for me many times. I know it's surprising, George, but a part of you really does love me."

I didn't respond. I only looked down at the table, concurring that he was correct.

"Let me show you something, George." Emmanuel got up from his seat and ran behind the bar.

I heard him fumbling through the back drawer and finally slamming it shut. He returned to the table with a pencil, highlighter and a piece of paper.

"You're going to love this," he said as he took the pencil and started to draw on the paper.

He first drew a circle and then a line down the center of it vertically to each end. He then drew another line horizontally to each end of the circle, crossing the other line. From there, he drew many more curved lines from side-to-side and up and down, until he finally created a sphere. It resembled a wire-framed drawing of the Earth with longitude and latitude lines.

After he finished drawing the lines, he turned the pencil around to its eraser and started erasing random shorter lines throughout the diagram.

Once he completed his drawing of the sphere, he picked a point between one of the lines, drew a small circle, colored it in with the pencil and then slid the picture over to me. "That's you," he said, pointing at the filled-in circle.

"What do you mean?"

"That's you. This entire circle is your life, and that

mark is where you are currently."

"My life?"

"Well, not really of course. The circle should be much more detailed, and naturally, this circle would look like a ball of light to the human eye. However, if you break it down and simplify it, this is what you would get."

"So, all of these lines are the directions I could take in my life?"

"Not just what you could take, but what you have already taken also. This circle shows all of the possibilities of your life."

I sat admiring the circle before asking, "So, is this what people mean when they say that God already knows what we are going to do before we do it?"

"Something like that, yes. God knows everything you are going to do, but he allows himself to not know the choices you will make. "

"It's a bit much. All of the lines and all," I said, trying to decipher the hastily scribbled drawing.

"Let me see it." Emmanuel took the paper and stared at it. "I guess it could be a bit confusing."

He looked at the drawing a few moments longer. "Hold on for a second."

Emmanuel flipped the paper over to the blank side and started to draw again.

This time he drew straight lines until he finally put them together to create a maze.

"Now, this should be better. Just look at this as a smaller section or a simplified version of that circle."

He turned the maze around to face me. "Okay, now go ahead and get to the finish line."

I took the pencil and started to make my way through the maze until I reached a dead-end and was about to turn around.

"That's it," Emmanuel said, placing his hand over the paper.

"What do you mean that's it?"

"Just that. You lost."

"How do you lose going through a maze? There is no such thing."

"With this maze there is."

"Why?"

"Because of sin," he answered.

Emmanuel turned the paper back over to the sphere he had drawn earlier. "See these lines that were cut off?" he said while pointing to the lines he had partially erased. "This is what sin has done. It has created paths that are cut short and incomplete. The sphere is no longer perfectly whole."

He turned the paper back over to the maze. "You've reached a dead-end, George."

I sat silent for a moment and then continued. "If God knows everything or every possibility as you say, then what's the point in me trying?"

"The point is love. It is for you to love God and to personally know that God loves you. Once that happens, you will have an understanding of your life's purpose and truth. You have to reassure your mind and heart that he alone is the God of truth. If you ever care to know the truth, then you must first find him.

"I know it may sound crazy, George, but the point of life is to simply love God. You can't fail if you love. The rest is just fulfilling what he desires of you next. And you must go to him to find out just what that is."

As I began understanding what Emmanuel was

saying, he continued. "Think of it like this. The creator of a maze sends you to find your way through that maze. The creator knows exactly how to get through the maze because he created it. He can never get lost or go in a wrong direction. The creator knows where you are going based on where you are headed. However, he allows himself not to know which direction you'll choose once you get to a fork in the path. It's up to you to make that choice alone. For instance, I knew that once you went left instead of going right, you were going to get to that dead-end. What I didn't know is if you would turn back around before it was too late, before you got to the dead-end. You made the choice to choose your route.

"Think of it as a test. The teacher can teach you everything you need to know before the test, but on test day, the teacher doesn't know if you'll pass or fail. However, he may know what you are likely to get based on your previous choices, participation and understanding of the subject.

"God *can* know all, but his true desire is for you to make your own choices without him. He only allows himself to know where each path leads. You make the choice on which you'll follow.

"Because of his love, he allowed your mind freedom to choose for itself. He knows you now like you know your child. When Mindy was a baby, you knew that if you held a stalk of celery and a pacifier in front of her, she would likely chose the pacifier.

"God doesn't prevent our decisions; he only inspires them. It's up to you to make the final choice.

"Think of this circle of life as a maze. God created it and yes, he knows every path and obstacle of this maze. Some are big and some are small. Some are complex and some are simple."

I interrupted. "Well, how do we know which path is right and which is wrong? It's a maze. There are no rules or strategy to follow."

Emmanuel took the highlighter that had been lying next to the edge of the table, uncapped it and colored in the maze from start to finish without ever going in a wrong direction.

After he finished, he looked to me and said, "Imagine a maze that already has the direction highlighted for you. A maze that is already completed and the only thing you need to do is follow the path of the light."

"The light, is that supposed to be you?" I asked.

Emmanuel answered with only a smile.

"If it were that easy, then why is it so hard? Why wouldn't everyone just follow you?"

"There are numerous reasons. People get distracted and lured into the darkness. They want to know more. They get impatient, convinced, curious or pressured into the unknown of what's down the other road or in that other direction. Some simply say they'll follow me later. They first want to get their life together before they can commit to me. Many people don't understand the simplicity of it all.

"The reality is that while everyone may start at different points, there is only one correct exit in the maze. In the beginning, everyone started in the light and on the right path and never knew what was beyond that path. Now, because of sin, everyone starts lost in the shadows of the maze and must find their way to the light. The only way to get to the finish line is to follow the torches that light the way."

"Torches?"

Emmanuel pointed to the highlighted area on the maze. “Think of this as torches of light that guide your path through the darkness.”

“How can I make sure that I’m successful? Is there some kind of trick involved?”

Emmanuel shrugged. “I guess you could say that the trick is to not be tricked off the path if you know it isn't your assignment."

"What do you mean assignment?"

"Well, some people are meant to come off of the path. That was the original purpose of the Church. It wasn't to just be a place of worshipping; it was meant to be a place of preparation and training.

“Think of the Church like an educational system. The students start as children and then work their way up to high school, then graduation and on to adulthood. Once they graduate, they go out into the world and produce based on what they have learned. Some continue into further education and become leaders and educators. That is exactly how the establishment of the Church was meant to function."

"Is the Church building up members and leaders so that they can ultimately fight Satan?”

"The Church doesn't need to fight Satan, George. They only need a torch. A torch is given to all believers to go out off of the path with their light and help those lost in the darkness. The battle is already won. The Church, or anyone for that matter, isn't fighting Satan. The present fight is for the mind. The war is within each person individually. Not between good and evil, but between desire and purpose.”

Growing deeper into the conversation with Emmanuel, I continued to ask more questions. "So if someone gets off of the path, how do they find their way back?"

"They can simply ask and I'll send the faithful with a torch."

"Why wouldn't everyone just follow you? Why won't we all just do what is right instead of effortlessly denying you?"

"It's not that easy, George. Some would consider that following the light is the gamble," Emmanuel replied in dismay.

"Does Mindy have a path to follow? I mean, do children have a maze also?" I asked.

"Not all children. Not even all adults have a maze or are judged based on a system such as this."

"How do we get chosen then? Do you just decide who is ready and who isn't?"

"No one is really chosen—it happens when a person gets to the point of accountability. This is when a person is able to discern his or her own religious choices, whether he or she chooses to accept sin, even after knowing that it is wrong. Naturally, most youth wouldn't comprehend making such moral decisions. That also includes any and everyone else who is incapable of making such choices through whatever mental disorder someone may have. Accountability happens at different ages and times for everyone.

"God's desire before sin was for all paths to lead to righteousness. Even after sin, he still desires that everyone follows that one passage of salvation and relationship with him. The only correct route to follow is the one that leads closer to God and further from sin. That path is very narrow and precise. There are no shortcuts. Truthfully, there are more roads to sin than there are to righteousness.

“It is your purpose to find the correct route to the truth. There are two ways to get to the right path. One is by asking me to come to you, and the other is by you coming to me. While everyone doesn't always ask for me, I always call them to the truth and the light. It’s up to them to listen and take accountability.”

As I reflected on all that I was learning, I glanced over to the vinyl that was sticking up on the edge of the table.

Emmanuel must have noticed me staring. "I should do something about that,” he said. “Hold on, I’ll be back." He got up, went behind the bar and returned with a roll of duct tape.

"Duct tape? Aren’t you supposed to be a carpenter?" I asked.

"That was the job in my past life," Emmanuel laughed. "Nothing like duct tape to solve a problem."

Emmanuel ripped off a piece of the duct tape and placed it on the vinyl. "See that? Perfect."

Emmanuel went to place the duct tape back into the drawer. As he returned to the table, I thought of another question. "Let’s just say that a man has never heard of Christ. Would he go to Heaven because he couldn't be held accountable?

"That answer is yes and no," Emmanuel answered. "An innocent man is more than welcome, just as a child would be, as they cannot be held liable. However, a guilty man would not make it based on his deeds alone.

“The question that you should be asking is if there are any innocent, guiltless humans throughout mankind. That answer would be ‘no.’ No guiltless, liable people exist on your planet.

“Because of their ancestors, humans aren't capable of being virtuous and noble on their own, and no one can get to Heaven without those qualifications.

“No one is held righteous simply by following the laws of the land. Righteousness comes only by following and believing in me. Every man has sinned; every man has fallen short of the glory of God.

“My Father accepts only two kinds of people in his Kingdom: those who are innocent and blameless and those who believe and follow me.

“If everyone lived according to the path that was designed for them, they would all come to know me. God’s presence is within everyone. There is a deep existence of life outside of this world and Universe that all will at some point encounter. That existence leads to a choice that leads to a path of finding the correct answer: me. If they haven't found me yet, it’s because they haven't made the right choices.”

"Couldn't we all just follow the Ten Commandments and be sinless that way?"

“No one is capable of completely following the commandments, and even so, the only way to truly obey the commandments is to follow me. Observing the law is not the same as having faith and believing in me."

"What if I just don’t want to follow anything or anyone?” I asked. “Let’s just say that I don’t desire to be a part of any religion, and I just want to live without believing in anything."

"That would be unrealistic, George. Following nothing means that you are following yourself and claiming yourself as lord of yourself. When you follow yourself, you follow sin. You can’t save sin from sin with sin. Everyone follows something and someone. If you don't serve God, then you are serving against him."

Emmanuel could see the discontent on my face. He continued, "My Father doesn't desire that you do wrong, but he does presume you will do wrong. You ultimately make the choices that you make. You make those choices based on your characteristics, education, motivations and situations. Who you are and who you associate with typically determines the choices you make.

"Sin isn't all that powerful, George. It isn't as strong as you may think it is. It can easily be overcome. To say that a sinful death is written at birth is to say that God can't overcome. God loves you much more than anything you could have done."

As my emotions grew, I asked, "How do I love him back?"

"Love is the fulfillment of the law. Because I am the law, if you love me, then you show love to my Father.

"You have given yourself problems, and God has given you a solution. There are many wrong paths, but only one right one.

"Love should never contain an expectation outside of its unconditional presence. The more you expect from God, the more likely you are to be disappointed in him. The moment you place God into your world of expectations is the moment you start to lose the true value of what love is."

"What is love exactly?" I asked curiously.

"I am love, and love is life and authority. The ultimate love is to give one life for another. In order to really love, you must love without an agenda of your own. The moment you walked into that market, you prepared to sacrifice your life for your wife and daughter. That was true love. Me giving my life for you is love. In return, I ask that you give your life to me."

We sat there together in silence, gazing out the window.

Emmanuel turned and asked, "Do you love and believe in me, George?"

I pondered before answering. "How can I say that I don't love you? If I don't, then I'm just a fool."

Emmanuel smiled and nodded. "You are fortunate. Blessed are those who have not seen me and still believe."

Six
THE WATER

Don't let your uncertainty stop you from getting to the other side.

I had been thinking deeply about what Emmanuel said before Cephas came walking through the back doors. In his hands were two plates filled to the brim with food.

As Cephas put a plate down in front of me, I grabbed the fork and knife and started slicing the eggs.

"George, would you like to wash up first?" Emmanuel asked.

I paused with the eggs two inches from my salivating mouth. "Sorry, I almost forgot," I said before I got up and went behind the bar to wash my hands.

After Emmanuel and I returned to the table, he placed his hands out in front of me and closed his eyes. Assuming he wanted to pray, I placed my hands on top of his and shut my eyes also.

Emmanuel began praying. "Thank you, Holy Father, for bringing us together for this meal that we are about to receive. To your glory we pray."

I opened one of my eyes and peeked at Emmanuel. "That's it?"

"What do you mean that's it?"

"You're supposed to be Jesus, I expect—I mean, I thought you would have a bigger and better prayer, something I haven't heard before, something powerful and earth-shaking."

"No, that's all," Emmanuel said, grabbing for a piece of bread, breaking it in half and handing me a piece. "Take, eat; this is my body broken for you."

I opened my hand, slowly accepting the bread, then turned it around a few times looking at it from every angle. "Should I just eat it?"

"What do you mean?"

I continued observing the bread for a little while longer before Emmanuel interrupted. "I'm just kidding, George. There is nothing special about this bread." He chuckled before taking a drink of water. "I just wanted to see how you would react if I really were like everything you believe me to be."

"I just don't know what to think," I said, placing the bread down on the table.

"What you may not know about me, George, is that I enjoy a good joke. Laughter is a healthy blessing."

"Laughter," I said with a smirk, remembering the blissful moments I had with my family. My thoughts quickly clouded with the memory of the shooting. "I guess in order to laugh, you have to forget about the pain. I won't ever forget those men—those boys—and what they did to me and my family."

Emmanuel placed his fork down. "You have to forgive others as my Father has forgiven you," he said earnestly.

"One day I may, but not right now. I just can't do it right now. It's still too real and personal."

"George, do you really understand the purpose of forgiveness?"

"Yes. It's letting go, forgetting about the past and moving on. Right?"

"That would be correct. However, you say you love me, but you can't forgive. It's offensive to say you love me and not desire to forgive others. To forgive means to love and to love means to forgive. Forgiveness should not be conditional. If you call yourself my follower, then it is your obligation to forgive.

"The sins you have committed against me are no less terrible than those who caused you harm. The forgiveness you extend should be immeasurable, just as my forgiveness is to you.

"You'll never truly find healing by holding on to selfish gratifications or vendettas. You shouldn't desire to be unforgiving, bitter and spiteful. What makes you believe that you are better than they are? Forgiving others isn't because of what *they've* done, but because of what *you've* done."

"Well, I still have things about myself I need to work on before I find that kind of compassion," I said stubbornly.

"That is all I ask, that you try." Emmanuel continued to eat his meal.

After a moment of nothing but the sounds of utensils moving and mouths chewing, I asked Emmanuel, "Why are you eating anyway? Why does

God need to eat? I assumed you wouldn't be hungry or desire food."

"Of course I'm hungry!" Emmanuel exclaimed. "All things in the flesh need to eat. Even plants and animals need to eat. Even the fruit and vegetables you desire need to consume water, earth and light in order to survive. Not just that, but I also love the taste of eggs," he said, leaning back and rubbing his stomach.

Just as we finished eating, Cephas arrived at the table and started collecting the plates.

Emmanuel kindly stopped him. "No, that's fine Cephas. I'll take those."

Emmanuel took the plates from Cephas' hands. "Take a seat, talk with our guest," he said and walked through the back doors.

Cephas sat down across the table, took off his suit jacket, stared at me and then crossed his hands. "Do you know who you are, George?" he asked in a stern manner.

"Who I am? What do you mean?"

"You've said you believe in Christ. If that is true, then you should know that you come from a very powerful family."

"Do you mean the Father, Son and Holy Spirit?"

"Yes," Cephas nodded. "Do you know who they are?"

"I believe I do," I said hesitantly. "The Father is God, the Son is Jesus and the Holy Spirit is—a spirit."

"That would be partially correct, but let me better explain. God the Father is life; he is the reason for it all. The Son Jesus is the love of God. The Holy Spirit is the strength and power by which all spiritual blessings and acts occur through God. Through the life of the Father, name of the Son and power of the Holy Spirit, there isn't anything that you can't do."

"So, God the Father has sovereign power over the Son and the Holy Spirit?" I asked.

"Yes, George." Cephas nodded his head slowly before continuing with his interrogation. "Do you know that you are created new through Jesus?"

"I know something of it, but I don't really believe that someone could actually become new. The whole concept is a bit over-exaggerated, if you ask me."

"Follow me." Cephas stood up from the table, walked slowly to the front door and waited for me to follow.

Without asking any questions, I stood up and followed him out the door of the diner.

Once we arrived outside, we stood on the small dirt path that lead up to the diners entrance, and Cephas asked me to look up to the sky. "You see the sun, George?" he asked, pointing to the sun, which was hidden behind the shifting clouds. "The sun helps to produce new fruit, not new seed in an old fruit. Believing in Jesus does not upgrade you to be a better man. Instead, it creates you to be a new one. To become a fruit, you must lose the seed of your mind and create a new one. You cannot become a new fruit until you break out of your old seed. Your old mind must die before you can be reborn. As it dies, so shall your old desires and habits."

"I thought Emmanuel said that we couldn't get a new cup."

"George, your mind, body and spirit are very different from one another. The cup that Emmanuel is referring to is your spirit. The seed I am speaking of is your mind. Your mind is what must be made new as it controls what you do with the body. In order to fix your mind, you must first fix your spirit by allowing God to access it. The Spirit of a man passionately yearns for a relationship with God. If you will feed your spirit with the Word of God, then your spirit will feed your mind with knowledge and purpose. As your thoughts change, so will your actions."

Cephas and I gazed at the sun in peace before I interrupted. "Why did God do it? Why did he send his Son? Why does he care so much about us?"

"The reason you don't really understand it is because you have never really loved anyone the way God loves you. Even the love you have for your family will never be enough to understand. Because you don't understand his love, you will never truly understand how or why he loves you."

Cephas reflected in thought and then chuckled before continuing. "I heard a young man once try to describe God's love to his younger brother. He used a simple idea, but in the end his brother fully understood the sacrifice Jesus made.

"The young man related the death of Christ to the story of a hit-man. He told his brother, 'Let's say that you are older and have a son. Not just any son, but a son whom you loved dearly and one to whom you gave everything you had.

'One day, your son calls you and he curses you out, tells you that you are worthless, that he no longer cares for you and he denies knowing you. He does this often, all because he feels you won't give in to his desires, desires which you know are bad for him. Nonetheless, he's turned to a wicked path of destruction and says that he wants you out of his life for good. Your son eventually follows the wrong crowd and plots to use everything in your family name to plan an attack against you.

'In that anger, you kick your son out of the family and throw him into the streets where he has to fend for himself without the authority of using the family name as a protector.

'Your son doesn't learn from his mistakes and he continues to follow this path. One day, someone puts a hit out on him because of a bad deal he made.

'The only thing that can save your son's life is for another life to be given in his place. Someone has to sacrifice in order to save his life. Not just any sacrifice, but the sacrifice of a life with greater value.

'Now, because your other son loves his brother, he agrees to sacrifice himself for the sake of his sinful, rebellious brother being allowed back into the family.

'Once it is done, out of respect for your good son and for the love of what he did, you tell your sinful son that if he ever wants to speak with you or gain his inheritance in the family, he has to love and worship his brother who sacrificed his life for his sake. If he doesn't respect his brother's sacrifice and death, then you can't respect or accept him back into the family.'

"Isn't that the simplest story that you have ever heard?" Cephas nudged me with his arm.

"It actually is," I said with a grin. "You're saying that the good son was the ransom because the corrupt son couldn't save himself? It's a story of love."

"That would be correct, George. What's worse is that the sinful son didn't even know he was in trouble. In order to appreciate the sacrifice Jesus made, you must first come to the realization that

Jesus is mightier than you."

Cephas continued to bask under the sun and clouds. "It's beautiful," he said in amazement.

"Walk with me, George." Cephas said, taking his attention from the sky and walking toward the side of the diner.

As we arrived around back, I noticed the shed with the blue truck. There was a large lake with a boat dock beyond the grass that I hadn't noticed before because of the night sky on my first visit out back.

As we moved closer to the old wooden dock, I was amazed at how divine the scenery was. Greenery and trees stretched across the opposite side of the lake, and the warm clouds covered the colossal mountains in the distance, like something I had expected to see only in a painting.

In the middle of the lake I saw a small wooden fishing boat. "What's that boat doing out in the middle of the lake?"

"That's where the best fish are," Cephas replied.

As I tried to figure out how they got to the boat, I saw a paddleboat behind the shed and realized they must use that boat to get to the other.

"Cephas, do you have the same powers as Emmanuel?" I asked.

"What sort of powers are you referring to? I can't save lives, if that is what you mean."

"No, not that. But can you part seas and move mountains, things like that?"

"That's not a power of Jesus, it's a power of the Holy Spirit. As long as you have the Holy Spirit, you yourself can do these things."

"Okay, so God the Father can do all of that also, I assume?"

Cephas looked at me, puzzled. "Do you know the difference between the Father and Son? Do you understand the relationship between the two?"

"Somewhat, maybe," I replied.

Cephas explained. "Just as you and your wife are one, the Father and the Son are the same.

"They are of the same nature and essence. Just as you give authority to your wife, the Father gives authority to the Son.

"To your children, you and your wife are one. When your children ask for something, they may first go to your wife, and if she deems the request worthy, she'll then ask you to make the final decision. Because you trust and respect her, you will likely go with what she agrees or tell her to use her best judgment.

"The relationship between the Father and the Son are like that of a marriage. She is a part of you. Together you are one. Likewise, while the Father and Son aren't physically one, their authority is as one."

"Their authority over the world?" I asked.

"Yes," Cephas answered.

"What or who exactly is the Holy Spirit? Is it a person or a spirit? I've read somewhere that the Holy Spirit is a being."

Without answering my question, Cephas walked to the edge of the dock, untied his shoes and then removed them. Once he removed his socks, he rolled up his pant legs to right below his knees. He then bent down carefully, sat down on the edge of the dock and placed his feet in the water. "Join me," he said while splashing the water.

Once I removed my shoes, socks and rolled up my pants, I sat next to Cephas and placed my feet in the water.

"See this water, George," Cephas said, looking at the water and gently caressing it with his feet. "The Holy Spirit is just like it. Without it, there wouldn't be life. Everyone needs it, and when they don't have it, they struggle to survive, and eventually they die. It is the genetics by which all living organisms are created and how life sustains itself. While many people may take it for granted, it is indeed the only thing that matters.

"Life was created by God the Father, and he blessed everyone with the Holy Spirit. Man doesn't appreciate it as the blessing it is. The authority you are capable of, you will never truly fathom how almighty and powerful it is."

"Is it really that simple? Is the Holy Spirit really just a form of energy?" I asked.

"The Holy Spirit isn't just an energy, but it's like the deoxyribonucleic acid within you, or what you may know as DNA." Cephas smiled. "If you know anything about DNA and genetics, then you know that it is transferred from father to son and can easily replicate itself within and through the bloodline.

"The Holy Spirit is the power and authority by which spiritual assignments are accomplished. It's a spiritual power gifted by a royal family. That family includes God the Father and God the Son. You have power because of who they are and because of their family name."

"Aren't the Father, Son and the Holy Spirit all one being? The Trinity, right?" I asked confidently.

"Or family," Cephas replied.

"How is that even possible to be three-in-one?"

"In order to understand the relationship between them, you need to know of them as a family. The

Father is in the Son, the Son is in the Father and the Holy Spirit is within them both. What connects the Father and the Son is that they share the same bloodline and DNA. That connection is the Holy Spirit."

I smiled back at Cephas before continuing with another question. "If the Holy Spirit is what allows me into Heaven, will sin cause me to go to Hell?"

"The Holy Spirit doesn't earn you a right to Heaven. Believing in Jesus is the only access to Heaven. Sin can't take away something it never gave you. The only way to lose your inheritance is by the one who gave it to you—Jesus. Denial of Jesus is the only way to lose your ticket into the Kingdom."

I sat in silence for a moment, pondering on all that Cephas had said while I kicked the water in the lake. "So how else is the Holy Spirit like water?" I asked.

"The Holy Spirit is like water in that it never dies. While water may lose its form, it never demises, but transfers. I can't thoroughly explain how the Holy Spirit looks, as you can never see it with your physical eyes. It can only be seen in the spirit, but it exists all around and within you like the air you breathe.

"Let's say that the Holy Spirit is like the bloodline of kings and rulers and the Almighty Creator of the most omnipotent Kingdom there is. The Holy Spirit is not just *any* bloodline, but it's a royal bloodline. Within that bloodline is power and authority over nations and all of the world and Universe. The Holy Spirit isn't just discernment, but it's the power and authority by which God the Father and God the Son are connected. Through the Holy Spirit, there isn't anything that cannot be done, because within the

Holy Spirit is the Father and the Son, which are life and love.

In order to enter the Kingdom of God, you must be a part of the family. All family members must be created of the life of God, love of Jesus and sovereign power and authority of the Holy Spirit. If you are missing any of those qualifications, then you will not be allowed into the Kingdom."

"So, God the Father and God the Son are connected because of their blood, and the Holy Spirit is a part of the Father and Son because it is within them also as it *is* the blood. That is how the family works?"

"That is exactly how the family works, George. However, don't think of the Holy Spirit as mere blood. That was just an example to help you understand. Understand that it is a spirit and what is in the DNA of that spirit that makes it holy.

"The power of the Holy Spirit is what keeps your Earth spinning and the sun shining and the plants growing. Without it, you couldn't exist.

"Every human on Earth has the Holy Spirit formed into their spiritual genetics at birth. The Father first created man by combining life with the Holy Spirit, and he breathed them into human beings out of his own spirit. Everyone has those four gifts of God: you can all move mountains, part seas, walk on water and heal the sick.

"Jesus came in the form of man and relied only on the power given to every man. He didn't come with a shield for skin or guns for arms or a brain 100 times the size of your own. The things he did are the things you can also do. It's up to you to truly learn how to use the gifts given by the Holy Spirit for all that it is."

"So, Adam and Eve corrupted the spiritual bloodline?" I asked curiously.

"That would be correct. Once man experiences sin, the holiness of his spirit is blinded to him. While the spirit was able to see, the Holy Spirit was blinded by the awareness associated with only the spirit. The Holy Spirit can only be activated by the presence of Christ."

"Why wouldn't it be that Satan corrupted us instead of Adam? He is the one who brought the awareness of sin?"

"Because you didn't come from Satan. The only reason that you are sinful is because you allow Satan, not because you are a descendant of Satan."

"How do I use the Holy Spirit that I'm given?"

"In order to use the Holy Spirit within yourself, you need Jesus' authority, which comes from God. God has to accept you back into his family before you can inherit what is in the Kingdom. The only way to be accepted is through Jesus. Once you have him, he will provide you with the direction needed in order to gain access to the Holy Spirit that is within you."

"So, is that what being filled with the Holy Spirit means? Being filled with the blood?"

"The purpose of the Holy Spirit is to fill you and transform your desires and heart into the likes of the Father and Son. As you become a believer and a follower in Jesus, the Holy Spirit within you grows because of the discernment given by Jesus. Through Jesus and by way of the Holy Spirit, God can communicate with you. It works almost like a walkie-talkie. God has one, and you receive yours through Jesus. If you don't have yours, or if yours is turned off or broken, you will never get the message or you may only get a part of the message.

"The Holy Spirit is strongest within you when you are a child because at that moment your mind allows you to desire higher authority to direct and lead you. Unless your mind becomes like that of a child, you will not enter the Kingdom."

"That happens at a different age for everyone, right?" I questioned. "That's what Emmanuel said earlier."

"The age when you willingly reject authority is when you diminish the Holy Spirit in your life. At that moment, you have chosen to make your own decisions. Unless you choose to follow Jesus as a child follows authority, you will not enter the Kingdom. If you are looking for an age, then I'll tell you that most lose their childlike benevolence by the age of eight."

"Wow!" I said. "I think my daughter Mindy lost all of hers at two."

Cephas and I both laughed before he continued. "As a follower of Christ, you establish a relationship with the King of Kings and within a family that is richer and more excellent than you can ever imagine."

"So, if I'm not a member of that family, I will lose all of the power and authority that is within that family name."

Cephas nodded his head and looked back out to the lake. "The life of a follower of Christ should be filled with the fruit of the Holy Spirit at all times. The Holy Spirit is the reward for loving and believing in Jesus. It is a deposit and your ticket back into the Kingdom, guaranteeing your family inheritance."

"So, what's the difference between the two? Holy

Spirit and spirit?" I asked.

"A spirit is life, and the Holy Spirit is power and authority.

"Every living thing has the spirit of life, but not all living things have the Holy Spirit."

I looked up into the clouds. "Thanks, Cephas," I said. "You've really helped me understand."

While I continued to gaze out at the mountains, I felt the wood from the dock lift up from under me. As I looked down to see what it was, I saw that Cephas was gone.

"Cephas!" I yelled, looking behind me on the other end of the dock.

"Here I am!" I heard a voice say from in front of me. Looking to see who it was, I noticed Cephas there about 15 feet ahead, standing on the water.

Cephas walked to where I sat on the dock. "Would you like to join me?"

I looked at him wide-eyed. "Can I—Can I do that?"

"What type of lover are you, George? Are you a believer or a follower?"

"What do you mean?"

"Do you simply believe in the idea of Jesus' existence, or do you follow, participate and desire to be like him? If you are a follower, then do you desire to serve God, or do you desire for God to serve you?"

I paused and thought for a moment before answering. "I don't know exactly. I know what type of follower I want to be. I want to be the kind that serves God."

Cephas smiled. "Give me your hands, George."

I placed my hands on top of Cephas' as he stood

in front of me.

"Lift both of your feet up and then place them on top of the water slowly," he said as he carefully helped me.

I placed my foot on top of the water, noticing that the feeling was like something I hadn't expected.

"I don't feel any water," I said.

The water felt as if it were silk on a carpet-like surface.

"Now stand up," Cephas said.

I stood up tall on the water, but moments later the lake's surface beneath me broke apart, and I was immersed under water.

Flailing my arms, I felt Cephas grab me and help me to my feet, on top of the water next to him. Clutching onto him, I tried to shuffle back over to the dock, but he stopped me. "Don't let your uncertainty stop you from getting to the other side."

Still breathing heavily and soaked in water, I looked to Cephas. "Let me go."

As he slowly let go of my arms one-by-one, I stood on top of the water. Placing one foot in front of the other, I began to walk my way toward the boat in the middle of the lake.

When I looked to my side, Cephas was there and I said with a smile, "So this is how the Holy Spirit works?"

Cephas patted me on the back. "You've always had it in you, George. However, how the Holy Spirit works isn't as important as why the Holy Spirit works."

When we arrived at the boat, we got in and sat down.

Smiling and laughing, I asked Cephas, "How did

you end up coming to God?"

Cephas turned and looked toward the mountains. "My brother and I were fishing one afternoon at the Sea of Galilee. Somehow, Jesus found us and he called us to be led by him. Ever since, I've followed him."

At that moment, I became numb with shock as I realized who Cephas was.

Seven
THE MAKER

Many people know me very well, but few believe in me, and even fewer follow me.

Still soaking wet, I grabbed the first piece of cloth I saw lying on the floor of the boat and began drying myself.

"You might not want to do that," Cephas said. "I use that to clean my catch."

I stopped, sniffed the foul-smelling cloth and threw it back on the floor. "Thanks for letting me know."

Taking off his collared shirt and exposing his t-shirt, Cephas grabbed for some leeches and attached them to a fishing hook.

"Are you going fishing?" I asked.

"Yes, *we* are going fishing," he answered, wrapping a leech around the hook.

"Not me. I don't know the first thing about fishing."

"Yes you do, George. You said you're a marketer

right?"

"What does marketing have to do with fishing?"

"Fishing is pretty much the same thing. Bait and hook. How do you go about catching a new client? What's the process? Give me an example."

"Well, I research the industry and company and then put together a plan based on that research. Once I pitch the idea, that's generally it. I wait for the client to decide."

"See, George, it's the same thing as fishing. Prepare your bait, hook it and then catch. That's all there is to it. You know exactly how to fish."

Cephas placed a separate fishing rod in my hand and went back to preparing his.

Struggling to put my bait on the hook, I turned to see Emmanuel approaching on the surface of the water. He carried a red and white cooler.

"Hey! You made it!" he said, smiling. "Looks like someone fell in," he said, noticing my wet hair and clothing.

Emmanuel came aboard, grabbed a fishing rod and then sat down next to me as Cephas sat at the tip of the boat.

"So what have you two been talking about out here?"

I looked to Cephas who was peering out at the lake. Realizing that he wasn't listening, I answered Emmanuel. "I learned what the Holy Spirit is."

"*What* the Holy Spirit is? It's *who* the Holy Spirit is."

I became confused. "What do you mean? I thought it was power and authority."

"Yes. However, the Holy Spirit is also my Father and myself. Think of it like your last name. Is your family name a thing or a person?"

"I guess it is a person," I said pondering.

Emmanuel continued. "Either way, you learned what the Holy Spirit is capable of. That's what matters. I guess old man Cephas still has it in him," Emmanuel laughed, looking over to Cephas who was still watching the lake.

"So how was it?" Emmanuel turned and asked me excitedly.

"How was what?"

"Are you going to make me beg?" he asked, laughing. "How was the walk across the lake?"

"It was good."

"Good! That's all? You should be out there still running and jumping around like a child."

"I'm running and jumping on the inside," I said jokingly.

Emmanuel laughed and finished preparing his hook. When he finished, he positioned his rod to hang out of the boat next to Cephas', and then he gazed out into the distant mountains.

I readied my bait as best I could, placed my rod next to Emmanuel's and sat down, waiting for someone to start a conversation.

After waiting and nothing but the sounds of birds and the gentle ripple of the water, I asked Emmanuel, "What are we waiting for?"

Without turning toward me, he replied, "The water and sun aren't quite right yet. Enjoy the scenery, George. There are many things beyond man to be thankful for."

While Emmanuel and Cephas focused their attention on the glassy water, blue sky and snow-capped mountains, I kept looking over to Emmanuel in hopes that he would notice me. I had so many more questions to ask.

Emmanuel looked at me from the corner of his eye. "Can I help you?"

"I didn't say anything. Are you reading my thoughts?" I asked.

"Now, why would I want to do that? Are you thinking something you shouldn't be thinking?"

"No, but I do have a question."

"And what would that question be?"

"Not really *one* question, but I just want to know more about you. I know a lot about life, but not much about you."

Emmanuel turned toward me. "What do you want to know about me?"

"I don't know. What do I tell people about you? When people ask, what should I tell them?"

Emmanuel contemplated as he looked back out at the mountains before answering my question. "Tell them to not just believe in me, but to also follow me."

"What does that mean?"

"It means that what a person knows isn't exactly what that person believes, and what that person believes isn't always what that person follows. Many people know me very well, but few believe in me, and even fewer follow me."

"How does someone go about believing in you? Isn't it hard to just follow someone like you, someone they haven't met or really don't know much about? I'm sure you often see the struggle."

"George, to know me is to know yourself. By searching for the truth in who you are, you will eventually find me. I am the source of all truth.

"If someone hasn't found me, then they haven't

found their purpose either. If you genuinely want to know me, then search for your own purpose. By searching for your purpose, you will find me. By finding me, you will find you. Without the pursuit of purpose, you will never find your place within the world.

"Often times, those who believe they are in search of me are only searching for physical evidence that I exist, rather than a heartfelt belief that I exist. Of the countless prayers I receive, most are from men and women looking for a God who caters to them. The reality is that I didn't come to get anyone's approval as some may think. I came to offer them *my* approval.

"I've seen the heart of so-called followers search for new rules and rituals instead of a personal relationship with me. I don't understand why it's so difficult for man to comprehend that I'm a simple God. I haven't asked for much at all. I only desire what is capable of every man to give. Nonetheless, they've changed me to meet their personal appetite, and they have tried to manipulate me into providing unscrupulous blessings.

"They tell me 'tomorrow,' but their tomorrow must be today. Instead of getting their first, I get their leftovers. Instead of giving me all of their time, I get the time that no one else desires of them. To many, I'm not a God at all. I'm a routine or a habit. I'm comfort and tradition, rather than a personal God."

Emmanuel paused and thought. "What makes me so unworthy, George?" he asked while continuing to gaze out at the mountains.

I sat with my mouth half-open, not knowing if he was asking a question that needed an answer.

Cephas turned from facing the lake and asked Emmanuel, "Lord, could I please sit next to the young man?" he said, bowing his head.

Emmanuel got up, and then he and Cephas carefully shuffled around one another until Cephas sat next to me and Emmanuel sat on the opposite side.

Cephas turned to me and said passionately, "George, people need to understand that they can't want short-term commitments with long-term benefits. Loving God should be a lifestyle and not just determined based on a person's feelings at a certain time.

"God didn't send money, gold, romance, diamonds or oil as salvation for man. He sent his Son. Jesus is the only way. It is not enough to just know of Jesus; you must also have a personal relationship with him. No one is saved by the faith of others. No one is forgiven by doing certain deeds, saying certain phrases or talking a certain way.

"To know Jesus is to give up everything that doesn't benefit your relationship with him. Knowing him means that you must also be willing to give up all that you have for his sake. If following Jesus doesn't cost you anything, then you probably aren't following him correctly.

"You can't have a conditional relationship with God. His desire isn't to give you money and a nice family or to help you live up to the standards set by your mind.

"God doesn't want you partially or just during the night or morning or afternoon. He doesn't just want you on a certain day of the week. He doesn't want you to just believe. He wants you to follow.

"Many people have made the commitment to

believe, but they haven't made the commitment to follow God. Just as the body is meaningless without the mind, believing is meaningless without the commitment to follow. To have faith, you must follow *and* believe. These two work together."

"Isn't it difficult for some people to love God if they are living poorly or simply in a bad situation?" I asked. "Aren't we all just a product of our environment?"

"Not at all, George. You are a result of your relationships. Even if you have no home and are living in a box, you should still praise God. Genuine happiness and peace come from him. If you build a relationship with God, then no matter what the situation or environment you are in, you must continue to praise and worship him. Your love for him shouldn't be conditioned on whether he brings you worldly peace. It should be because he brings you inner peace."

"Why do I always feel like I need so much more then? If God is supposed to be enough, then why do I and others still desire more things?"

Emmanuel looked at me and answered. "No matter how much wealth or how many relationships a person has, everyone is ultimately in search of peace. I am peace. I am what everyone is subconsciously in need of. Many people use drugs; some use relationships; others use wealth, and there are plenty of other provisional comforters that are used to try and create the peace that only I can give. Many people try to replace their need for peace with pride. Nevertheless, they'll never find happiness through these other temporary satisfactions. It is not your spirit that is asking for more; it is your sinful mind and desires, which seek a physical comfort.

"My promise was never to be fulfilled in the form of worldly wealth, but through greatness in Heaven. I came to redeem man from the curse of sin, not to help him live a comfortable life here on earth. While I may be known as peace, I did not come to bring peace. I came to bring division amongst believers and nonbelievers."

"So what is it to truly believe? Even now, I believe in you, but I don't really know why. I don't know if I do because I saw you or because I just believe for no reason at all."

"That is a struggle that everyone has, George," Cephas replied. "However, you shouldn't believe in Jesus because you've seen him; you should believe because you have a relationship with him. Your belief should come from you knowing him personally. It doesn't take physical evidence to love something or someone. What it takes is for you to look into your own heart and find truth and purpose in whatever it is that you love. Once you find truth and purpose, there you will also find God and love."

I pondered before asking Emmanuel another question. "Now that I believe in you, what can I expect now? How will my life be different as a believer?"

"To believe is to take action," Emmanuel answered. "Believing in itself is not an action. However, to believe in me is to also have faith in me. If you have faith in me, then you must take action on that faith in order to truly believe. As Cephas just said, faith without action is worthless because faith is expressed through action. Faith sees, speaks, hears, thinks and acts. You cannot genuinely believe and not produce good works."

"It's time," Cephas said as he turned around and grabbed his fishing rod.

"What are we doing? What am I supposed to do?" I asked.

Cephas handed me my rod. "This is called still-fishing. Just watch me and then you try. It's fairly simple."

Cephas took his rod and then gently cast the line into the lake. "That's it. Go ahead and give it a try," Cephas said with a big smile.

As I tried the technique, I asked, "Is that it?"

"That's all there is to it," Cephas answered.

Once Emmanuel joined us, I continued asking him questions while we waited for the fish to bite.

"Okay, so if I do believe in you, what kind of action are you expecting me to take?"

"Well, George, the only action you need to take is to follow and represent me as close to your capabilities as possible."

Just as Emmanuel finished answering my question, Cephas pulled in his first catch.

"That was fast," I said.

Cephas pulled in the fish and placed it into the cooler before unhooking it. "I would love to say that I'm just that good, but it wasn't my technique that caught the fish. It was the timing. Had we started fishing when we first got here, the timing would have been wrong. Don't you know that the world revolves around the clock? If you want to fulfill your purpose, then make sure you're following the right clock. Not your own clock or your friend's clock or your money's clock. God desires that everyone follow him and believe in him, but you also have to make sure the time is right. If you don't, you'll never hear him because you'll either be too early, or you'll miss him because you're too late."

"How do I know when the time is right?"

"Just ask, keep listening and meditate on the Word of God. When you know God, you'll know when he's speaking to you," Cephas said before dropping his baited hook back into the water.

I turned to Emmanuel who was smiling and pulling in his catch also.

"Why is it that sinners are successful? I never understood why some sinners have more money and are happier than people who follow you? Shouldn't following you equal success and not following you mean failure?"

Emmanuel pulled in his next fish and answered, "That is exactly what it means. However, your idea of success is different from the success I am here to reward you with. My Father is the one who rewards based on doing and believing.

"For instance, if you do a good deed, my Father will reward you whether you are a believer in me or not. This is why you may see many nonbelievers who have many riches and possessions. That reward is based on what you do, but not what you believe. While this may bring worldly success, it will not produce true peace or hold you a place in Heaven. Only by believing and following me is that possible. God judges good deeds just as he judges wrongdoings.

"Everyone lives by the same laws of the land. My Father is the one who offers the rewards, gifts and talents. I only offer a way. I am not a reward given by a mystical heaven. I was given to you by my Father.

He has provided you with everything you need in order to live successfully on Earth and to enter Heaven. He is the true one who blesses man.

"If you believe in me, nothing at all may change in your physical world. I've come to change your desires and your mind. The only way to produce good fruits of this land is to first plant the seed where you want it to grow. That is how it has always been.

"God still abides by the laws he created before I came to earth. Life is still based on your harvest. Worldly success comes through good deeds. Heavenly success comes through me. If you want oranges, you plant an orange tree. If you desire apples, then you plant an apple tree. You cannot plant an apple tree and expect oranges. God has given you exactly what you need in order to get whatever it is that you desire. If you desire to be with me in Heaven, then you must plant my seed within your spirit."

"So what you're telling me is that I don't really need to tithe in order to enter Heaven?"

Emmanuel laughed. "That's what you got from what I just said?"

Still laughing, he responded, "Tithing is considered a good deed. It's the same as donations, charity work or offerings. If you tithe, then my Father will reward you. However, tithing does not guarantee a place in Heaven. I don't reward you for tithing or save you a place in Heaven if you tithe. Tithing is simply giving to the Church to help spread the Gospel.

"You are saved by faith alone. However, faith should inspire good works. Your works, including tithing, should be the result of your faith. Being born-again means to first believe in me and then to live your life as close to me as possible. The fact is that you can't truly believe in me and still be of your old bad habits or ways.

"There are many ways to be successful here on earth, but there is only one way to enter the Kingdom. I don't promise success by believing in me, but I do promise eternal salvation and a place in Heaven."

"So. . . I'm not understanding. Do I need to tithe?" I asked, still confused.

"George, I never gave the command or law to tithe. My teachings only speak of giving freely. Give, as you are able. So, no, tithing isn't a requirement or a commandment. Tithing isn't about giving money. It's about giving to the Kingdom of God. It's about helping to expand my name. You can do this either by tithing money, time or other items of benefit. How can you desire to follow me, but not desire to give toward my cause? Why do you expect to reap from my wealth, when you have not sowed anything for me?

"To love me, you must be transformed into a new creature. The new you should have new desires. Giving should be a natural desire of yours once you have been transformed as my follower. As you are transformed, your heart shall change and giving will not seem like a requirement or task, but it will be a joy."

"I got one!" I yelled, pulling the wild fish into the boat. It landed on the floor and started flapping around, flicking water on everyone."

"Are you going to pick it up?" Cephas asked.

I grabbed at the fish and tried to hold on as it

kept slipping through my hands. The boat rocked back and forth, and I almost fell into the lake before Emmanuel grabbed my shirt and steadied me on my feet.

Cephas captured the fish and placed it into the cooler while I sat back down.

"Thanks for catching me, Emmanuel," I said exhausted.

Cephas responded. "You might fall, George, but even when you do, God will never let you hit the ground. It's his natural instinct. We've fallen many times and are undeserving people. However, God somehow still loves us. He loves us so much that he gives and rewards even a sinner."

"Then why did you let me fall in the water the first time?" I asked Cephas.

"Because I'm not God," he laughed. "Your brother can only help lift you up. He can't protect you from your fall, only God can do that. Look to your brother for help, not for protection."

Cephas placed another leech on my hook, tossed it back into the water and handed me the rod.

"Let me ask you, George, what's your weekly schedule?" asked Cephas.

"I don't usually have a set schedule. I guess I wake up and whatever I have to do that day, I go ahead and do it. Normally that's some kind of work, of course. I might have a presentation to practice, or it might be a day of research or writing."

"Now, throughout that week, what do you plan to do to spread the good news of God? How are you going to help expand his name? How are you going to follow his footsteps throughout your life?" Cephas paused.

"Many people say they believe. However, when you look at their weekly routine, the time they spend with and for God is only a small percentage of how they spend their time. Don't just contribute your prayers and financial support, but be a part of God's movement. God desires for you to do more than just believe and support those who believe."

"I haven't really thought about that, I guess. Maybe I could go to church and see what positions they might need help in."

"That's a good start. Do you know what kind of church you are going to attend? What about outside of the church? What if you don't like the church leaders? What if the church doesn't have air conditioning? What if your family doesn't like it? What are you going to do if the church isn't comfortable enough for you with cushioned seating, big television screens and flashing lights?"

"I don't know. I guess I would go to another church."

"I'm asking you this because many people say they believe in Christ, but when believing involves losing some comforts, they forget their love for him. They forget who it is they follow. They start following whatever is easy and convenient. They choose their leaders based on popularity or who can put together the best performance. Don't desire or be attached to worldly comfort. Choose your leaders based on who has chosen God as theirs. I've been following God for a long time now, and I can tell you, while God is easy, following him can be tough at times. You must forget about how others view you and concern yourself only with what God desires of you. If your church, family or friends don't accept you, then release yourself from them and follow only God, for he accepts all.

"If you have no money to your name, no clean clothes or a home, many may leave you and say that they never knew you. However, God will love you at your best *and* at your worse. He doesn't expect you to look a certain way, nor does he desire you to have wealth. He doesn't care about what car you drive or the home you live in. He doesn't care if you can sing, if you can dance, or if you can play a sport or write a song. God loves all, and he especially loves those who love him. He wants everyone to join him in his Kingdom. It's up to you and only you to choose to follow him. Your worldly possessions won't ever impress him. Being the wealthiest man in the grave means nothing. Heaven doesn't reward you based on what you have. Its reward is based on what you believe."

"How do I choose what to do next then? Is there anyone in the world who I can follow? Is there a particular religion or preferred church or other temple?"

Cephas threw chum into the water, attempting to get the fish biting again. "George, don't follow religion because it feels right or because someone suggests it to you or because of your heritage. If it doesn't help you grow, then it's not for you. Don't try to be accountable to the religious leaders, but be accountable to God. Go wherever your heart tells you and wherever you can be spiritually filled. Once you fully comprehend your purpose, you'll be able to know exactly what God wants you to do.

"Choose your church home and family based on who is following the same spiritual journey as you.

Follow so that you can one day lead, not so that you can find comfort in following. In the end, you are responsible for you, no matter whom or what religion you decide to follow."

"What if I make a mistake? Should I just repent and it will all go away?"

Emmanuel answered, "Repenting simply means that there is awareness and regret for your wrongdoing. It lets God know that you are trying. You will be forgiven, but you must also correct the matter. Nonetheless, the healing of sin is much longer and painful than the forgiveness I offer you. I didn't come to remove sin, but I came to offer an alternative to sin's effects."

"So, is it just over after I sin? Do I just go to Hell if I forget to ask for forgiveness?"

"George, sin can't prevent you from entering Heaven, just as it didn't allow you access to Heaven. The only way to enter Heaven is through believing in me, that I am the truth and the way. The only way to be denied from entering Heaven is to deny that I am the truth and the way.

"If sinning were powerful enough to pull you from Heaven, then it would also be powerful enough to allow you in. If you believe in me, I will always believe in you, George. However, you must repent for your sins if you do happen to sin.

"I don't expect you to lose the weight of sin overnight. Just as if you desire to lose physical weight on your body, losing the weight of sin will take time, exercise, dedication and knowledge until it becomes habit. Nonetheless, if you try and believe in me, then sinning cannot remove you from your place in Heaven.

"I stated before that trying is all that I ask of you. If you don't repent, then that means you aren't trying."

"What if it *is* an accident— sinning?" I asked. "What if I just didn't think and it just happens?"

"If that is the case, George, then you must repent. There are moments when sinning is done not by choice, but because of human nature. However, if you believe and follow me, then you should have fewer of those accidents. If you forget to repent, then you have forgotten me.

"However, to love me is to have grace, and to have grace means to have time. Accepting me allows you time to correct your sinful nature. My love is not like that of a man that I will leave you after you offend me. I love you even after you forget your love for me. Having the Holy Spirit doesn't change you physically, but it allows you to know spiritual truth. With my Father, you are graced under an unconditional love unlike anything that man can offer you.

"No matter how hard you try, you will never fully comprehend the love that my Father has for you. He loves you for who you are, were and will ever be. His love is greater than any of your past, present or future sins. The only thing that can remove you from his grace is not believing in me.

"It's inevitable that you will sin. As a man born to sin, you will never be strong enough to fully deny sin. However, through believing in me, you will see the truth of your ways and the faults of your sinful nature. My Father knows who you truly are and once you believe in me, the Holy Spirit will open your eyes to truth and lead you to the correct path designed for your life.

"Nonetheless, there will be times when you fall or close your ears to my teachings. However, don't for a second think that I am ashamed of you or that I don't accept you. Don't beat yourself up after you sin. Repent and move forward and away from sin and continue your walk with me. My patience and understanding are unthinkable. You will never truly love me to perfection, and I don't expect you to reach that level, but I do want you to try. Trying is my only true desire of you.

"The only way to prevent yourself from sinning is to find value in something you love greater than sin. With me, your life should grow to a point at which you shouldn't *need* to repent.

"The reality is that without love, there is only sin. You must place me above your sins, George. That is the only way to avoid those potential accidents."

After Emmanuel and Cephas finished answering my questions, I grew an even greater appreciation for the sacrifices that Jesus made for the sake of my life. I knew then that God was more powerful and worthy than I had ever thought he was. At that moment, I knew that no matter how hard I tried, I would never be able to truly understand the perpetual love that God has for me.

Humbly, I turned toward Emmanuel and asked, "What is sin?"

Emmanuel paused and pondered for a moment before answering. "To sin, is to not seek God and follow his direction.

Most of what you may think is sin, is nothing of it. God has a different plan for everyone and it's the reason you must not judge your brothers or sisters.

What may be sin to you, may not be sin for what God has planned for them.

Everyone must have a personal relationship with God, and he alone will determine what is and is not sin for that individual."

Reflecting on all that I had learned, we each sat introspectively relishing the scenery gifted by God as we continued to fish.

Eight
GRIND THE BEANS

You can't believe in something that you doubt.

After we finished fishing, each of us walked back to the diner and cleaned ourselves up before lunch. Cephas gave me some spare clothes. Then Emmanuel and I sat in the diner chatting while Cephas prepared the meal.

"George, do you now have a better perception of who I am?" Emmanuel asked.

"I think I do. I knew before that you wanted everyone to be successful and prosperous, but I never understood the true meaning of those words. I only knew of what was possible within the world. Now I know that your definitions are broader than what I could see.

"My hope is that I can make your desires my own and follow you wherever you lead or ask me to go. I understand now that you are not just a voice of reason, but you are a friend and God. You are the only way, the answer of all answers and the truth of all truths. To know you is to know me and to know me is to know you."

Emmanuel grabbed my hand, which was resting on the table, and shook it. "Today I'm proud, George. However, you must remember that just because you believe in me, doesn't mean that you follow me. Don't promise me. Show me."

"Could I ask you something, Emmanuel?" I said nervously.

"Of course. What is it?"

"While I cherish these moments with you, and I hope not to offend you, I would like to go back and see my family. It's daylight now, and I believe help may be easier to find if I went now."

"I can help you back, George, but are you sure you want to go?"

"With the earthquake and not having seen my family or knowing of their condition, I would just like to be there for them through this moment."

"I understand. Yes, I'll help you back to your vehicle."

Silence came over the table for a while before Emmanuel asked, "As we wait, could you tell me more about your family?"

"Of course," I said eagerly. "Well, Carol and I actually met while she was in college and I lived in the same city where she was going to college. She had been working at a fast food restaurant, and one day around lunch, I saw her there. I just couldn't stop myself from being the creepy guy staring at her.

"I didn't say anything that first day, but I kept coming back almost every day that I could afford it, just so that I could try to spark up a conversation. I had never actually figured out how to talk to her because she only took the orders, and the lines were usually long. Getting into a good conversation was difficult, so I hardly said much of anything.

"Nonetheless, I had been going to church around that time, and one morning before service, I saw her. She was right there heading into my church. I sat in the back telling myself I was going to say something to her that day.

"After service was over, I went up to her and asked if she lived in the area and if she worked at the restaurant. She answered and that started a nice conversation that led up to me asking for her phone number. Ever since then, we haven't been apart."

"How did you propose to Carol?" Emmanuel asked as Cephas presented our meal: the fish we had just caught and some warm vegetables.

Cephas set the plates down, and Emmanuel and I washed up and then prayed over the meal before continuing our conversation.

"I actually got Carol to plan her own surprise engagement. Of course, she didn't know it, but it was the only way I could really make it a surprise.

"Once I had decided to ask her to marry me, I needed a perfect plan to make it memorable. I knew several months before I proposed that I wanted her to plan her own engagement. I just didn't know how I was going to pull it off.

"Just around the same time, her brother Nick had a birthday coming up. Nick and I were very close, so I figured I could use his birthday as a way to arrange the entire thing.

"I had been away on a business trip out of state. One night while speaking with Carol on the phone, I asked her if Nick's birthday was coming up. Once she confirmed, I suggested that she throw him a surprise party. After she thought about it and realized that he had never had a surprise party, she said it was a great idea.

"After I had planted the idea, I suggested getting a large venue and just having a nice party and inviting everyone.

"Once I had Carol planning the party and sending out invites, I ordered a cake that said, 'Carol, will you marry me?' The cake decorator had been a mutual friend of ours, and she knew of what I was trying to do. The funny thing was that after I ordered the cake, Carol contacted her and ordered the same cake, except her cake said, 'Happy Birthday Nick.' I told the decorator to just make them both and let Carol pick up the one she ordered.

"By the time the event was near, I had told almost everyone about the day, so I was able to get almost everyone involved in setting everything up. I even let Nick know of what was going on.

"That day, the plan was to first bring out the birthday cake at the beginning of the party so that Carol could see it sitting on the table and think that we would be cutting it later.

"I remember being so nervous about the whole thing. I just wanted it to be perfect. I had purchased the ring, kept it in a safe and pulled it out often to practice what I would say and how I would say it. I even cleaned the ring a few times whenever I thought it wasn't shining enough. There were so many questions going through my head up until the moment. I was sure that she would say yes, but it was still one of the most nervous times of my life.

"When we finished dinner and were ready to cut

the cake, I had the server walk into the room backwards as Carol began to panic because she couldn't find the candles for Nick's cake. As she continued to scramble, each of the guests started singing 'Happy Birthday' until Carol finally turned around. Everyone stopped singing, and it took her almost an eternity to actually look at what the cake said.

"Once she did see the cake the I had for her, with tears in her eyes she looked down to me kneeling, and I asked her, 'Will you marry me?' She immediately struck me in the shoulder and almost pushed me off balance. After she said, 'yes,' I jumped up and gave her a giant hug."

Remembering the look on Carol's face that night, I looked out at the forest through the window with a huge grin on my face.

Realizing how much I missed her, I turned toward Emmanuel and asked, "Are you ready to go yet?"

"Sure, we can go now," he said before rushing more fish into his mouth and wiping his hands with the cloth napkin.

As we stood up from the table, Cephas walked out from the back.

"Are you leaving now?" he asked.

"Yes, I am. I'm going to go see if I can get some help back on the road and get my car towed. Thank you for taking the time to talk with me, Cephas. It has been a joy," I said before giving him a hug.

"Your clothes aren't finished drying yet, do you want to wait for them?"

"No, that's fine. Please keep them. Do you want yours back? I can wait for mine if you do."

"No, that's fine, George. I will see you again."

Emmanuel and I left the diner, and once we arrived at the forest, Emmanuel grabbed a stick from the ground and used it to help move the hanging branches from the path ahead of him.

The direction in which we were traveling seemed to have been different from what I remembered. However, I figured he knew where he was going, so I followed him without asking questions.

After we had walked for almost 20 minutes, I grew tired and worried that we were lost. "Are you sure this is the right way?" I asked.

"Yes, I know exactly where you came from." Emmanuel continued walking through the path, waving his stick to move tree limbs and tall weeds.

Minutes went by before we arrived at the bridge over the small creek I remembered crossing on my way to the diner. Once I saw the bridge, I was relieved to see that we were heading in the right direction.

After another 10 minutes of walking, I could see the entrance back to the road.

When we left the forest, we were met with the sign that said, *A Taste of Heaven.* I smiled with relief once I read the sign.

Once we got to the location of the accident, my car was nowhere to be found. I hadn't even seen any glass or tire skids anywhere around the light pole.

Anxious, I asked, "Where is my car?"

Emmanuel remained standing on the side of the road in the grass and didn't answer until I grew angry and agitated. "Where's my car?" I yelled.

"There is something you need to know, George."

"No! You said you would help me. Where is it? I

need to see my family!" I cried before falling to my knees with my head to the ground.

I calmed down before asking Emmanuel, "Please, just tell me. Am I dead?"

"Your spirit is very much alive."

"Then what are we doing here?" I asked, drying the tears from my reddened eyes.

"I brought you here because you asked me to. Not only that, but I knew it was the only way you would accept what I am about to show you."

"Was there ever an accident?"

"No, George. There was never an earthquake either. I will explain it all once we get back to the diner. That is if you care to know the truth."

"Is any of this real? Are you real?"

"I am as real as you believe me to be."

"Is my family safe? Please, I need to know! If not, I beg that you help me back to them."

"They're safe, George."

I got up from my knees, wiped myself off and looked down each direction of the road before heading back in the direction I came with Emmanuel.

Walking back through the forest, I felt weak and lifeless knowing I wasn't going home. I stopped and sat down on a tree stump, and Emmanuel turned around and walked back toward me.

"Why have you stopped walking?"

"Because there isn't anything to walk for," I said calmly while bent over with my head on my knees and tears running down my face.

"George, do you still trust me?"

"I don't know what I trust or believe any longer. I feel like you knew. Like you knew and you just wanted me to go through it anyway. What was the purpose of bringing me here and putting me through this? Was it because you enjoy seeing me in pain?"

"George, your pain doesn't indulge me. It is through your faith that I receive pleasure. Clearly, you have lost faith in me. You question my doing and rest when I ask you to walk. Do you wish me to leave you here? Do you not seek understanding of what really is? If you want truth, then follow me. If you desire to weep in sorrow, then you may stay and find your own way."

Emmanuel turned and continued walking back in the direction of the diner.

I waited nearly 15 minutes before standing up and wiping my tears. Once I was ready to walk back to the diner, I went in the direction I had seen Emmanuel walk. Somehow, I managed to have gotten lost for more than an hour before I finally made it back to the diner.

I arrived at the door exhausted and knocked. Cephas slowly came walking from the back and opened the door. "Do you have a reservation?"

"No, I—"

Cephas interrupted. "Please take a seat and wait," he said, pointing to the bench next to the door.

A few minutes later, Emmanuel came to the door, and I got up from the seat and wiped myself off as he came outside.

"Please, sit back down," he said as he took a seat next to me on the bench.

"Why should I allow you back in, George? Is this what I should expect from you? One moment you say you desire to follow me, but the next you let your emotions lead you away. Do you know what leads man away from me more than anything?"

"I don't know," I said with my head down in shame.

"Emotions, pride and opinion. I don't desire, nor am I a God who seeks to comfort what you feel.

"Let go of your feelings. That is when you will truly find me. I shouldn't have to compete with what you want or feel. Call me selfish, but what I'm offering you is much greater than your personal feelings.

"What do you have to say for yourself? What is your explanation for knowingly disobeying anything that I ask of you?"

I answered unsure. "I don't know. What do you want me to say?"

"I want you to apologize. Repent for what you have done. Not just that, but mean what you say and try with all your being to make yourself better. The only feelings that should cover you are my own feelings.

"George, you will never be strong, not until you learn how to overcome your weakness. You can't believe in something that you doubt. There is no such thing."

I looked up, turned to Emmanuel and said earnestly with tears in my eyes, "I really am sorry. I have no excuse for what I did. Please forgive me."

"It is done," Emmanuel said smiling. "Now, you haven't told me about your daughter Mindy."

Confused on how easily Emmanuel had accepted my apology, I wiped my eyes and stuttered, "Sh-she's five now, but she's a good girl. What do you want to know about her?"

"Tell me a funny story about Mindy. I'm sure you have plenty," Emmanuel asked enthusiastically.

I still couldn't fully understand the sudden change in Emmanuel's emotions, but I gained my composure and continued to think of a story.

I laughed while thinking of a moment and then started telling it to Emmanuel. "Once, when our family took a trip to Florida. Our car rental company was located a few miles away from the airport, and we ended up taking a taxi back to the airport at the end of the trip. I sat in the front, and Carol was in the back with Mindy, who was in her car seat.

"We arrived at the airport, got our bags from the trunk and realized we were running behind on time. We ran into the airport to check our bags, but luckily, the check-in line wasn't too long. We checked our bags just in time before we headed to security.

"For some reason, whenever Mindy went through the security scanners, she kept setting off the alarm. We took off her shoes also to see if they were the problem. She was only two at the time, so of course she didn't have anything on her.

"Carol and I finally remembered that Mindy liked to stick things in her diaper. We looked in and found a small key ring with four keys that she had stuffed in there.

"We laughed once we realized what happened, but then Carol asked me if they were my keys. When I told her no, we both got confused about where Mindy had gotten them.

"Nonetheless, while we tried to figure out where the keys came from, we heard someone yell, 'hey!' As everyone turned to see who it was, we realized it was our taxi driver. Carol and I looked at one another wide-eyed and realized then where the keys came from.

"The funny thing is that we still haven't figured out how exactly she got the keys. Either she's the best pickpocket in the world, or she just saw them lying around somewhere. For all we know, she might have taken them out of the ignition while we were getting our bags from the trunk!"

Emmanuel and I laughed as I finished telling the story.

"That's a great story. Mindy really is special," Emmanuel said. "Can I show you something George?"

"Of course, what is it?"

"Come with me inside."

After arriving inside the diner, he told me to stand and face the glass window that stretched across the front of the diner.

Cephas walked into the room and stood in front of the door.

"Don't be afraid," Emmanuel said, standing in front of me and placing his hands on the sides of my head. "Close your eyes."

As I closed my eyes, Emmanuel started whispering a prayer.

After he finished, he asked me to open my eyes. When I did, I looked at him standing in front of me with a smile on his face.

"What happened?" I asked.

Emmanuel didn't respond and only continued smiling. I stared back at him, but through the glass window behind him, I noticed moving shadows. When I looked pass Emmanuel's head, I saw Carol and Mindy playing in the front garden of the diner.

Without thinking, I immediately sprinted toward the door before halting after noticing Cephas guarding the entrance.

In awe, I approached the glass window slowly by crawling onto the booth seat. I couldn't believe my eyes. “Is this real?” I asked Emmanuel without turning to look at him. “Are they really here?”

Emmanuel didn't answer.

I stared at Carol and Mindy joyfully, and tears welled up in my eyes. As I noticed a little girl playing with Mindy, I asked Emmanuel, “Who is that?”

Emmanuel answered softly, “That’s Addie.”

“Is that a friend of Mindy’s?”

“No, George.” Emmanuel walked over and placed his hand on my shoulder. “It’s your daughter.”

“That’s not my daughter,” I laughed.

I turned back toward the window and pointed. “Not Mindy, that girl right there. The shorter one with brown hair. Who is that?”

“That’s your daughter, George. She’s the daughter you lost two years after you had Mindy.”

I turned back toward the window and stared at the little girl. Tears flowed down my face and fell to the floor as I remembered the miscarriage Carol and I had a few years ago.

“How? Can I go out to meet her?” I cried.

“No, George. You must remain here.”

After accepting Emmanuel’s response, I asked, “Can they see me?”

“No, they only see the lake and dock. This is the place they created within Sheol.”

I turned and faced Emmanuel. “Why? Why are they here? Are you showing me this because I'm dead?”

“You know the truth already, George.”

I turned back toward the window and placed my

hand on the glass. "I was just with them yesterday. I had breakfast with them. I felt them. I spoke with them."

"You have to let them go. They passed away a long time ago. You have to move on."

I pulled away from the window and cried intensely before turning to look back at Emmanuel. "Why are you putting me through this?"

"The shooting was real, George. It happened. You have to let them go. It's the reason why you are here. Your spirit needs you to move on."

As the reality of their death struck me painfully, I banged my fist against the window and yelled. "No, they can't be dead!"

When I finished weeping, I opened my eyes and could see Carol, Mindy and Addie all looking up in the direction of the diner. I turned around to Emmanuel. "Did they hear me?" I asked frantically while turning back around and continuing to pound on the glass.

Mindy came walking toward the diner and stood a few feet in front of the window.

I bent down and placed my hand where she was. "What is she looking at? Can she see me? Could she hear me?"

"She feels you, George. She feels your presence, but she feels it coming from across the lake and in the mountains. She misses and desires you to be here with her. They all do."

I knelt, coming almost face-to-face with Mindy and watched her shortly before she turned back around and ran to Carol and Addie.

"Is this Heaven? Are they in Heaven?"

"It is only the first Heaven. They are in Sheol. It

is the resting place for souls before I return and bring them up to the Kingdom of Heaven with me. No one enters the Kingdom until my return."

After nearly 10 minutes of gazing out the window, Emmanuel walked over to me. "Please turn around, George."

Once I knew that it was time to let them go, I removed my hands from the window and turned around to face him. He placed his hands over my eyes and after finishing his prayer, he wiped my tears and asked me to take a seat on one of the bar stools.

I grabbed a napkin and finished drying my face before he asked, "Can you tell me the story about Addie?"

As Emmanuel mentioned Addie, I remembered seeing her precious face. Joy filled me as I realized that I had nothing to worry about.

"Where did she get the name from?" I asked Emmanuel.

He chuckled before answering. "She actually got it from Mindy. Carol named her Addison, and Mindy could never accept it," Emmanuel said as he and I both laughed.

Just then, I remembered that Carol had come up with the name Addison many years ago before the miscarriage.

"So, her name is Addison," I said, remembering her beautiful face.

"Well, you might want to check with Mindy about that," he answered. "Mindy renamed her Addie, and everyone else just followed the boss."

Emmanuel and I continued to laugh about Mindy's keen personality before he said, "Now, tell me about Addie, George."

I pondered for a moment before remembering the heartfelt story that surrounded Addie.

"As you know, Addie was our second child after Mindy. It was three months into the pregnancy, and Carol was so excited. She started coming up with names, emptied the guest room and made it the new baby's. She decorated and painted the walls pink. I asked how she knew it was going to be a girl, and she said she just knew. I remember having to put everything in the attic and garage while she stuffed the room with more pink and other baby things.

"After a doctor's visit a few months later, Carol had called me crying and saying that something was wrong. The doctors could only tell her that she would lose the baby. I remember not knowing what to do, but Carol prayed every night and day as often as I could remember. She even had the church pray over her in hopes to save the baby's life.

"Nonetheless, a few weeks later while I was away on a business trip out of the country, Carol had an emergency visit to the doctor because of a pain she had felt in her abdomen. That visit was when they told her the baby hadn't survived. They never explained what happened or why we lost the baby, and I think that made it even worse for Carol.

"I wasn't there, but I remember her telling me that she asked to hold the baby after they removed her. The hospital staff cleaned the baby and gave them privacy for as long as she needed. She told me how she kept her most of the day and named her then. There was so much emotional pain she felt after losing Addison. I was saddened of course, but I could only imagine what it must have been like for her to have done it alone.

"During the weeks to follow, Carol seemed overwhelmed with grief. She would go to bed crying and wake up in the middle of the night crying. She spent hours searching the Internet for information and explanations of what happened and why she lost the baby. I didn't know if she would ever find happiness again. I had joined an online support group and read books, searching for advice on how to help her through the process.

"With time and support, we both were able to make it through the devastating experience."

After I finished telling Emmanuel about Addie, I thought of seeing Carol and Mindy with her, and I remembered the joy in their eyes. "I'm glad they are together," I said delighted.

Nine
TAMP THE COFFEE

A man will never understand how to love until he first knows what love is.

"Do you want me to leave you alone for a moment, George? Maybe some privacy? You've been through a lot today," Emmanuel said.

"I don't know," I answered nonchalantly.

"How about you go outside for a moment," Emmanuel suggested. "Get some fresh air and come back in when you're ready."

Emmanuel got up from the table, patted me on the shoulder and then went through the back doors of the diner.

I sat thinking for only a moment before going out front of the diner. There I stood, staring introspectively at the spot where my family had been. I remembered their exuberant faces and recalled the days after the heist that took their lives.

I awoke from a coma in the middle of the third day after the shooting. I remember the hysteria I was in after realizing I couldn't move my legs. I yelled for Carol and instead was surrounded by the blue scrubs of two hospital nurses.

"Mr. Henry, please. Calm down," one of them said as she came and placed her hands on me trying to hold me down.

"Carol!" I yelled, trying to get up before being yanked back by the straps holding me to the bed. I struggled, trying to fight through the nurses and straps until a sharp burning pain caused me to fall back on the bed, weeping in agony.

"Mr. Henry. Relax. It's okay. You're in the hospital. You were in an accident. Just calm down and I'll get your doctor for you," the young nurse said before running out of the room.

Catching my breath and trying to lessen the pain in my back, I laid back calmly, hoping the hurt would pass.

"Mr. Henry, how are you feeling?" a pleasant female voice said. "I'm doctor Lowery. How do—"

"Carol. Where's Carol?" I moaned.

"Mr. Henry, I'm sorry," she said compassionately. "There was a bad accident, and Carol and Mindy didn't make it. I'm very sorry," the doctor said softly as she stood with her clipboard down, waiting for my reaction.

I remember not wanting to accept what she had said. Even after she later told me the entire story of the four gunmen and the market, I chose not to believe a word she said. I ignored and dismissed any discussion on the subject. After attending the funeral a week later, I never shed a tear and only convinced myself that their death wasn't real. When the reality of them being gone occasionally entered into my mind, I fought it in hopes of keeping the loving memories of my family alive.

I didn't know how to have a life without them. I kept them alive for as long as I could and hid it from friends and family when they would bring them up. Deep down I knew the truth, but I also enjoyed the peace and happiness I felt while living within the shelter of their memories.

Eventually, my health started declining, and I was unable to eat and could barely hold a coherent conversation. The doctor told me that the lower part of my body had been temporarily paralyzed due to a thoracic spinal cord fracture. I underwent two surgeries and seven months of rehabilitation before I returned home to living what I considered a normal life with Carol and Mindy. By the ninth month, I was back at work traveling and marketing.

"George," I heard a voice say from behind me. Emmanuel placed his hand on my shoulder as I sat crying, tears falling from my chin. "It's okay, George," he said as he got on the ground next to me and held me in his arms.

"I want my family back. I can't do this anymore," I cried.

"It's okay, George," Emmanuel whispered. "It's okay. They're home. You haven't lost them."

Once I became aware and realized that Emmanuel was cradling me like a child, I pulled myself away and wiped my eyes. "I didn't want to remember. I liked it the way it was."

"You weren't fine, George. A lie will only last temporarily. It's been a year since you lost them, and the reality is that it will never get any easier to let go.

Life has to go on. There will always be heartache and emptiness because of your loss, but you have to cherish the memories that you once had with them. Be thankful that they are together, and find peace in that. You need to release yourself so that you can move on to what you really need to do."

I got up from the ground, wiped the dirt from my pants and said sarcastically, "And what is that? Tell me, Emmanuel. What is it that you believe I need to do?"

Emmanuel stood up. "Let's go back inside," he said, walking toward the diner.

Cephas opened the door, and after Emmanuel stepped in, Cephas walked out and grabbed my arm. "I need to speak with you, George," he said.

I looked for Emmanuel's approval, but he had already gone through the back doors of the diner.

After I realized I was stuck with Cephas, I turned to follow him until he stopped and stared out at the forest.

He placed his hands in his pockets. "If you die today, would your life had been worth anything?" he asked without turning around.

I stood behind him and replied. "Maybe. I'm happy with what I've done."

Cephas turned and started walking toward the side of the diner. I followed.

"Life isn't about your happiness," he continued. "That is where many people have their biggest misconception. If you think God is here to make you feel good or to provide you with emotional happiness, then you have him all wrong.

"You are part of an immense group of people who don't know what God truly desires of them.

Your joy and satisfaction hold no essential relevance to that of God. He would rather you follow him and be miserable, than to not follow him and be happy.

"How you value your life and how he values it, are entirely opposite of one another. You want today, and he wants tomorrow. You want now, and he wants forever. You must be willing to lose everything for him. If you can't let go of your success, power or emotions, then you will never be able to say that you will follow him anywhere. If you aren't willing to follow him, then you should know that he has nothing left to sacrifice for the sake of you. He's given everything he has while you continue to hold to your worthless provisional things, hoping they will bring eternal happiness.

"Stop questioning God. Start questioning your simplistic life. You are the one who doesn't comprehend. You'll never understand the value of your life, not until you understand the value of his life."

I interrupted. "Then why—"

"Quiet," Cephas turned and said firmly. "You've talked enough nonsense for one day. Here you are with this opportunity to speak with God himself in the flesh, and you speak to him as if he's a weak man with no power over your soul. If you don't desire a relationship with him, then leave. Be dead to him. Stop wasting his time. You've come and gone repeatedly, and you speak to him as if you are the one to be desired.

"Your thoughts and desires are so minuscule and petty. You whine because your heart is broken and yell because you hate the truth. Somehow, through a love which I don't possess, God forgives endlessly, even to those who are undeserving. However, that gives you no right to disparage him as being weak and worthless.

"Your life is meaningless without him. If you desire to chase after the wind in search of your peace, then feel free to run through the forest. Go get lost in the woods trying to find your own way out. Cry when you get lost and spend your days and nights alone because you don't want the help of the one who created the forest in which you are lost.

"Leave if your desires aren't here. Curse God if that makes you feel powerful. I say these things because none of them matter. The day will come when you knock on the door and no one will answer, when you seek and peace won't be found, when you call him a friend and he will say he never knew you."

Afraid to say anything as we reached the lake, I waited for Cephas to speak again.

He picked up a stone and threw it into the lake. "A fool says in his heart that there is no God. Another fool says there is a God, but I choose not to follow him. Which fool are you, George?"

I answered hesitantly, "I-I'm not a fool at all. I believe in God, and I have chosen to follow him."

Cephas turned and studied me for a second, as if I were a pathetic waste of existence. He then turned back to the lake and threw in more rocks. I watched and wondered what he wanted from me. I knew that believing in God wasn't instant, and I was sure he knew that it would take me some time. I've heard stories of people taking years before they finally understood how to love and believe properly.

I waited a short while and built up confidence before speaking again. "What do you want from me?"

I asked.

Cephas paused from picking up more stones. "What do you mean what do I want from you?"

"You expect me to be a perfect follower of Christ when you know that I just started believing. Emmanuel didn't say he needed me to believe full-heartedly right now. He knows that it's going to take me some time. All that he asked of me is that I try as best as I can. He knows my heart."

Cephas chuckled. "God knows your heart. I've heard that many times. However, the funny thing is that you are right. God does know your heart, but you know nothing of it. What you believe about your heart and what God believes can't be compared. You might think you know, but you have no idea what your heart is even capable of.

"You believe yourself to be some mindless failure. You blame your lack of spiritual effort on your pitiful life, your ancestors, your love, your finances, et cetera. You know everything about who you are to yourself, but nothing about what you are capable of through God.

"You need to restore your mind in order to find out what you are. It is the only way to seek direction from God. You must lose your doubt so that you can find peace in awareness of him."

Cephas picked up a few more rocks and tried to skip them across the lake, but each one only fell straight down to the bottom. "Tell me, George. What is your purpose?"

"From my conversation with Emmanuel, it's to try."

"To try what?"

"To try and live according to God's will. Do what

he desires of me."

"And how are you going to do that? What's going to be your motivation? If you fail, then what? What if your car breaks down or someone you love breaks your heart? What if you run out of money and have to work all day at your job, will God have room in your busy schedule? You seem to know how to find an excuse to fail. Now let me see you find an excuse to succeed."

Cephas turned to face me before he continued. "My concern isn't whether you believe in God; it's whether you will always believe in him. If you have no idea how to release your emotions from the things of this world, then you will never be ready for the world that God has to offer."

While he returned to throwing stones into the lake, I pondered my answers to his questions.

"I would do whatever it took," I said confidently. "Of course I'll encounter problems, but when I get to those bumps, I'll be ready."

I went over to Cephas and placed my hand on his shoulder. "I'm going to do my best, I promise. I know it may not be good enough for you, but it is all that is asked of me. The truth is that I will never be good enough. He gave his life, and even if I gave my own, it would certainly not compare to the life of God."

Cephas smirked and nodded. "Lovely answer, George," he said before patting my shoulder and turning back around to find more rocks.

I picked up a few rocks and started skipping them across the lake one-by-one.

"Don't try to showoff, George," Cephas said while shaking one of the rocks in his hand. "I should skip this off of your chest," he joked. We both laughed and continued our conversation.

"Remember that you have a choice: to choose God or to try it on your own," Cephas said. "By not choosing him, you are choosing to be conformed to your life as it is. Yes, prayer is key to gaining strength and focus, but it is also needed as an acknowledgement of your limitations. You must pray to gain strength, and until you can follow him without thought, you need to take every moment you have to meditate on his words.

"The reality is that everyone sins. Trying to ask a man not to sin is like asking water to not be wet. If you focus on God and stop thinking about what you can do for yourself, then you'll be just fine."

"What do you think?" I asked Cephas.

"Think about what?" he said, continuing to look for new rocks to throw.

"How can I focus my attention on him? How can I love him like you do or like he should be loved?"

Cephas stopped searching for rocks and stood up, clearly musing. "That's a good question," he said.

"You know, George, a man will never understand how to love until he first knows what love is. Not just what others have done for him out of love, but what the actual word 'love' means.

"In order to love God, you need to first believe in your heart that he is the truth. However, if you don't know what the word 'believe' means, then you will never know what it is to truly believe.

"You must first educate yourself so that you won't be ignorant to his word. Without knowledge and definition, you will never know how to fully love him. By lacking interpretation, his words will never make sense to you.

"In order to find God's purpose for you, you must first understand what the word 'purpose' means."

Cephas pondered before continuing. "Don't let your enemy outsmart you. Not just the enemy that lives around you, but also the enemy that lives within you."

He showed me a small stone that he must have found near the lake. "See this rock?" he asked. "It may seem insignificant and puny, but if you understand what it is made of, you will know its true strength. With the proper power behind this rock, it can break or damage anything in its way. Create yourself, and your walk to be like this rock. Build yourself and your mind, and then watch God move you with his might."

Cephas handed me the rock, threw the rest into the water and walked back toward the front of the diner. "The issue with most people is that they don't know what they are capable of. Their lack of knowledge sets them up for an eternity of damnation simply because they don't understand the power within them.

"God knows what you are capable of. There have been many before you who have used your same excuses for not following his desires. He knows how you think and how you choose. He knows that you are incapable of perfection, but he also knows that you are capable of knowing what is right and wrong. If you simply make your decisions based on your knowledge, then choosing should be easy. If your knowledge lacks, then you need to educate yourself using the appropriate resources that will help you gain wisdom. Lack of knowledge as a believer is how an unbeliever wins the argument against you."

If you say that you are his follower, then you must represent him as such by being wise in his teachings. Without knowledge and education, you'll never know the true value of his words."

We sat down on the bench at the front of the diner, and Cephas turned to me, continuing, "You can only give what you have received. Not everyone is meant to do and know everything of the world. Do what you are best at and what you are gifted with. However, all creatures, including the plants and animals, have been gifted with the ability to learn. You have to use that gift in order to find your purpose.

"The community of God is very large and gifted, which is good, because you will never be able to go it alone. Find people like yourself and with your same desires to serve God. If you are good at and enjoy marketing, then do that. When you're doing it, make sure that you are doing it for the benefit of expanding recognition of the Kingdom and the glory of God.

"The joy will come in the morning. Don't worry yourself about whether you can afford it in terms of money or time. God will make a way and will reward fully. Don't allow doubt and foolishness to hold you back from your blessings.

"It's all deeper and yet simpler than you think it is. While following God may be difficult, loving him is easy. If you know you love him, then keep that in your thoughts as you proceed throughout your day. If you aren't willing to make sacrifices for him, then don't expect him to make them for you."

Cephas stood up. "You ready to go back in now?"

"I think so," I replied as I got up from the bench and followed Cephas back into the diner.

"I'll go to the back and get Emmanuel," Cephas said before I stopped him.

"Wait. I have a question," I said as Cephas and I both took a seat at the bar. "How did you do it? How did you make it so easy to follow God?"

Cephas answered, "More than anything, you must have faith. The fact is that I can't explain to you how to have faith. It's something that you must feel and know. Once you have it, even then it will not be easy to let go of your old self. My best advice is to never look back. Let go of the memories and emotional attachments created by the old you. Once you do that, you'll easily find your correct path.

"By letting go, you allow your spirit to be emptied of its old ways and filled with the new ways of Christ. Nonetheless, while the Spirit may forgive easily, the mind never forgets. Learn to control your mind by filling it with the Word of God and allow him alone to direct and lead you.

"God is jealous for you, and he desires that you follow him and him alone. By holding on to who you were before him, you can't fully dedicate yourself to being in a relationship with him. It's the same if you find a new wife. You would offend her by holding on to your past life and family. While she may understand that you have many emotional attachments, she expects you to let them go and let her in. You can't love your new wife and still hold on to your former wife. If you try, it will destroy your new relationship.

"You can't love two persons equally, just as you can't serve two gods."

"I think I get it now," I said. "I have to plug myself into God."

Cephas looked at me puzzled. "What do you mean?"

"Carol always said that God is like an electrical socket. The spirit is like an electronic that needs a plug, and God is what gives it the power. The only way to obtain the power of God is to plug your spirit into the power socket that God provides."

Cephas laughed and nodded his head. "Carol is a smart woman."

"Yes, she is," I said as a reminisced about her.

Cephas continued to chuckle as he got up from the stool, went behind the bar, grabbed a rag and started wiping the counter tops.

"Another obstacle you may run into is trying to figure out or understand who your ultimate Judge is. I'm sure you know right now that it is God, but many forget. At times, you may find yourself subconsciously desiring others to judge you based on your looks, intellect, popularity, finances and so forth. Be sure to remember that God doesn't care about any of that. He only desires that you love him and follow him."

Cephas finished cleaning and leaned over from the other side of the bar. "I'm only telling you all of this, George, because I don't want you to fail. I know it's going to be hard, and I'm sure you know also. However, you have to know why it is hard. The hard part isn't in loving God; it's in following him. You live in a time when no one wants to follow and everyone wants to lead. They all want to create their own destiny, rules and path to follow. Everyone wants to deem themselves as god instead of believing that there is someone higher and greater than they are. In following God and his path for you, you have to learn to position yourself second. You are addicted to loving yourself, your emotions and your comfort.

"Sinning is unavoidable. Don't let failure drive you to quit. Just remember that you aren't a sinner because you sin. Rather, you sin because you are a sinner. God loves the sinner and hates the sin. Nevertheless, there isn't a sin that God won't forgive. As long as you ask for his guidance and mercy, he will give it to you.

"If you try it on your own, you will only find that it is impossible to find peace within. Peace comes only through him and acknowledging that he is God Almighty. While loving him may seem complicated, if you truly love him, then all of those doubts, fears and confusions will evolve into peace. Once you find his peace within, you won't desire anything outside of it. Let God's love be your addiction."

I put my head down as I recalled a painful moment after the death of Carol and Mindy.

"What's wrong, George," Cephas asked.

I hesitated.

"Tell me," Cephas said concerned.

"It was several months after the shooting and my first time being back in my home without my family. I remember crying endlessly those first few days. I didn't function properly without them there. The silence of the house, Carol's clothes in our closet and Mindy's toys everywhere. I guess I expected it all to be gone along with them. That night was when reality first struck that they were actually gone.

"I walked into the bathroom, pulled out every pill in our medicine cabinet and placed them on my lap before I forced them all down my throat. I had hoped to kill myself that night. I remember thinking I didn't want to live without them. I felt I had no purpose after they left me. I only wanted to be with them, and I convinced myself that if I died I could either be with them again or I would at the least be out of the pain that I felt.

"I fell asleep that night after I took the pills, and the next morning I awoke unaffected by the drugs.

"Nonetheless, when I awoke, I heard Carol and Mindy's voice. I got myself up from the floor and hurried into Mindy's room. I saw her there, with Carol reading Mindy's favorite story. I knew they were gone, but I also knew I didn't want to lose them again. Since then, I've been living off their memories and even creating new ones with them. It might seem strange, but somehow it saved my life."

Cephas replied thoughtfully. "George, the whole point of life is trying to live. If you stop trying, then you've missed the point. Not only that, but by taking away a person's life, you're taking away that person's ability to try.

"God desires every person to live until he calls him or her. He will never call you to take your own life. You and everyone else in the world are birthed with a spiritual gift of life. He desires that you appreciate that gift and spread it amongst the world. If you understand that, then you know that your life is important and not just intended to benefit your personal desires, but to also help others in their walk.

"As a follower of Christ, you are called to expand upon your gift of life. You must play an active part in building up the Gospel and the Church and living as God's ambassador. You cannot do these things by taking your own life.

"The sin that you would be committing is in denying God's desire for you to live and grow for his sake. Any gift of life, whether poor, rich, weak, strong, healthy or sick, is far greater than a life in Hell. Nothing is worth giving up. By taking your own life, you are also taking the life of many others. Not because of what you've done, but because of what you could have done.

"Know and understand that God is the only thing worth dying for. Even so, he will never ask that you take your own life to be with him. He desires you to fight for him. If you don't die trying, then you've died for nothing."

Cephas came around to the other side of the bar and sat next to me. "You are very important to God's cause. Your life was worth the cost of God's one and only Son. Don't devalue yourself just because you don't know what you're truly worth."

"Thanks, Cephas," I said.

He smiled and said, "Would you cut off the branch you are sitting on if it were keeping you from falling?"

"Of course not," I answered.

"Then see God as that branch. The branch can exist without you, but you cannot exist without the branch. The next time Emmanuel tries to hold you, let him hold you for as long as he desires." With those words, Cephas walked through the back doors and was gone.

Ten
HEAT THE WATER

Life isn't about what you can see, it's about what you know and believe.

After Cephas left the room, Emmanuel returned minutes later. "Hey, George. Are you feeling better?"

I nodded. "I'm feeling much better actually. Cephas seems to have a way with words."

"Yes, he does." Emmanuel said, taking a seat across from me at the table.

"I'm sorry, Emmanuel."

He looked at me puzzled. "What are you apologizing for?"

"I'm sorry I didn't allow you to lead me."

"It's okay George. I'm used to it," he shrugged.

Without responding, I thought about how insignificant my apology must have been when compared to the billions he receives daily.

"I have a question to ask you," I said. "Earlier, you mentioned that my family was in Sheol. What or where exactly is that?"

Emmanuel placed his hand on his chin and then stared at me before answering. "Would a simple answer satisfy you? Or would you like to know more about the Heavens and Hell?"

"There's no reason to hold back now," I said excited. "I want to know all that you can tell me."

Emmanuel got up from his seat and went behind the bar. "Would you like some orange juice?"

"No, I'm fine. Thanks."

After pouring himself a drink, he came back around and leaned on the bar. "George, do you know where a person goes after death?"

"They either go to Heaven or Hell. Right?"

"What if I told you that Heaven and Hell were fairly close to one another?"

"What do you mean?"

"Well, when a person dies, their body goes to Qeburah. However, their spirit goes to Paradise or Hell, which is practically within the same region."

"Okay, but what about Heaven?"

"Paradise *is* Heaven. It's also known as Sheol." Emmanuel paused. "I don't think I can explain it to you as well as I can show you. There is some simplicity about it. However, it's also pretty difficult to explain."

After setting his glass on the bar, he went to a back drawer and returned with a pencil and paper.

He began to draw a large circle in the center of the paper. Within that circle, he left about an inch of space and drew another circle. Within that circle, he left the same amount of space and drew another circle. He then drew another circle with about half an inch diameter, placed it within the middle and colored it in. Altogether, he drew three circles and a dot in the center; similar to a dartboard.

Once he finished drawing the circles, he named each of them and placed the name within the open area between each of the circles.

Between the first and the second outer circles, he wrote *Sheol/Paradise/First Heaven.* Between the second and third circle, he wrote *Hell/Death.* Within the third circle and the dot, he wrote *Hades.* Then he drew an arrow and a line pointing to the dot and labeled it as *The Pit/Abyss/Lake of Fire.*

When he finished, he moved the paper to the middle of the table and leaned in to explain.

"These locations represent where people go once they leave their bodies and die in the flesh."

Emmanuel watched and waited as I examined the drawing.

Seeing my confusion still, he further explained the drawing.

"This is all within the Earth: Hell, Hades, Sheol and the Lake of Fire, which is also known as the Pit or Abyss."

"So Hell and the Lake of Fire are different?" I asked.

"Yes and no; the Lake of Fire is within Hell. However, Hell is not the perpetual place where sinners suffer for all eternity. That place is known as the Pit. The Pit is located within Hades, Hades is located within Hell and Hell is located within Sheol. They are different in that they are different locations. However, they are the same because they are both within Hell. They are just in different locations within Hell.

"Every location within this drawing is known as the Earth below or the Realm of the Dead. Imagine this being a sphere with layers, each layer being a different location. The first layer is Sheol, the second layer is Hell, the third layer is Hades and the inner core is the Pit.

"Hell and Hades are within Sheol. Sheol encompasses the righteous, and Hell encompasses the unrighteous. Together, they form what is known as the Realm of the Dead. Think of the Realm of the Dead to be like the Earth. The Earth has believers and nonbelievers that worship in different temples. While each temple is different, with separate meanings and purposes, they are all within the same Earth. As you may consider, the Earth is neither good nor bad, it is only a location that holds the good and bad. It's the same thing with Sheol and Hell being located in the Realm of the Dead.

"You have to look at all of this as if it were a state within your country. The state's name is Sheol, and within that state there is a city called Hell. Within Hell, there is a building called Hades, and within that building, there is a location called the Pit. They are all within the same location, but are very different."

"What is the difference between each of them? I know what Hell is, but what is Sheol and Hades?"

Emmanuel sat back in his seat and answered. "Sheol is the first Heaven, and Hades is the place within Hell that holds the unrighteous."

"What about Qeburah? Where is that located? Is that in Hell also?"

"Qeburah is not within Hell. It is only a grave that is created by man. Think of Qeburah as the grave in which your body is laid to rest," Emmanuel answered.

"So, Qeburah is within the surface of the Earth and Sheol and Hell are within the core of the Earth?"

"Yes!" Emmanuel snapped his fingers. "Your body rests within Qeburah, but your spirit lives within Sheol. Going to the Realm of the Dead is only the first death, which is the death of the body. The second death, which is the death of the spirit, comes after the final judgment for those who are in Hades. The righteous spirits in Sheol have no second death. Through believing in me, I have removed their spirits from the second death. After the second death, your spirit will either be resurrected into the Heavens above or thrown into the lake of fire."

"Are people burning in Hell right now?"

"There is only burning within the Pit located within Hell."

He continued, "Think of Hell as a jailhouse, and think of Hades as death row within that jailhouse. After death row, there is the electric chair. Think of that electric chair to be like the Abyss, or Pit or Lake of Fire, whatever you want to call it. This is where the spirits burn. No one enters the Pit until Judgment Day. The righteous and the wicked will be judged the day when I come. Once they have been judged, they will either be let into the gates of Heaven, or thrown into the Pit of Hell."

"What's the point of having multiple places within the Realm of the Dead? Why not just allow people to go to Heaven or the Pit right after they die?"

"Because, they need to know why they are there, George. They need to learn and understand the reason for their judgment, whether good or bad.

"If you were to go to the Pit, wouldn't you want to know why you are there? The same if you were to go to Heaven. Eternal salvation comes through me on Judgment Day, not through death."

"Can the spirits within each of those locations see and talk with each other?"

"Of course," Emmanuel answered. "But only by the choice of the righteous in Sheol."

"How does that work then?"

"As mentioned before, the unrighteous are in Hell. Hades, which is within Hell, is where the unrighteous and fallen angels are imprisoned until my return. Like a prison allows visitors, if the righteous desire to venture to Hell, then that is their choice. A demon in Hell cannot touch my followers. Just as I have walked through Hell and Hades, so may my followers. Even in death, my Word can still be heard and taught."

"You've been there before? To Hades?"

"Upon my death, for three days, I entered the Realm of the Dead in the heart of the Earth. I ministered to all, even to those imprisoned. That was the day of the first judgment. That day I ministered to everyone in Sheol and in Hell, those who had followed the laws of Moses and those who were imprisoned."

"Why did you go to the Realm of the Dead? Why not just go up to Heaven?"

"Sheol *is* Paradise. It's the first Heaven. All go to the Realm of the Dead upon their death, George, even the righteous."

"What about the saved believers? Did you allow them to Heaven?" I asked, finding myself being engrossed by the conversation.

"Before me, there were only righteous and non-righteous spirits of those who followed the laws of Moses. Those that made it beyond the laws and into Sheol were very few in number compared to those in

Hades. Nonetheless, with my first coming, the gates of Sheol were opened, and the righteous were released to the Heavens of God."

"So your second coming is the rapture?"

Emmanuel laughed. "Something like that. Through my second coming, the spirits of the righteous will be lifted into the greater Heavens. Some of those spirits will rise from Earth, and others from within the Realm of the Dead. If anyone believes in me, they will be taken up to the high Heavens upon my return. Do you understand now, George? You seem to have a lot of questions."

I laughed. "I just want to understand it correctly, as I've heard many theories on the subject."

I paused for a brief moment before asking my next question. "Will I know who my wife is once I get to Paradise?"

"George, you will see whoever you desire to see. If you know your wife's spirit, you shall certainly be able to find her in the Heavens."

"You keep saying Heavens. Are there multiple?"

"There are many Heavens. Sheol is known as the first Heaven or Paradise. However, when I speak of the Heavens, I am referring to the greater Heavens beyond the Earth. The first Heaven will be destroyed along with Hell in its entirety once the Earth has also been destroyed after the final battle. The first Heaven is only a temporary resting place until my return. Through the destruction of the Earth, so will be the destruction of Sheol, along with Hell and Hades. However, the Lake of Fire will burn for all eternity."

"Okay, I understand now," I said. "When a believer lifts into the Heavens, will the body go with them? I know you said we will only see spirits, but what happens to the body?"

"The body will remain in the ground where it first came from, and the spirit will return to the Heavens. The body is built of only dirt and sand used to protect itself and to sustain the physical being. In the Heavens, there is no need for the body. It belongs to the Earth. What is of the Earth will remain with the Earth. What is of the Heavens will be given back to the Heavens. I don't desire your body; I desire the spirit within it. If it does not belong to me, it will not be given to the Heavens. In that same manner, if you have given your heart and spirit to the world, then they together will burn in the Abyss upon my return and judgment."

Emmanuel finished off his drink, washed the cup and placed it back inside the cabinet before continuing.

"George, there is a network of energy that flows throughout all living things. That includes the plants that grow, the sun that shines, the clouds that move and the air that you breathe. It is all connected through a stream of energy known as life. If you could see the world as a spirit sees it, you would see more than a pretty face or a beautiful landscape. Imagine seeing the world for what it really is. While you may think your wife and daughters are beautiful now, wait until you see them in the spirit. A good spirit is one of the most angelic beauties ever known. Life isn't about what you can see, it's about what you know and believe. If you could comprehend and embrace the world for what it really is, then you would understand God, and God's grace is more glorious than anything you could imagine.

"Your true self is what you are created of and not

what you are created with. You must beautify your spirit in order to gain God's attention. To love him, you must love all of his creation. Once you have succeeded with that, your beauty will shine brighter than all of the stars in the sky. To be unrecognized by God means to be left for the Abyss.

"The thoughts of a man shine through his spirit. It is why a sinner must change their sinful thoughts in order to be all that God desires of him or her. Don't let your spirit be an infection to others, and don't let others corrupt you. The result is that you alone are responsible for the life and energy that you produce. A soiled spirit has no place within the Kingdom."

I rested on what Emmanuel said and thought of more questions to ask.

"Sorry if I keep asking questions, but is there any way that I or someone else can communicate with those who are in the Realm of the Dead? I mean people who are living, can they talk with people in the Realm?"

"I see you're asking more complex questions," Emmanuel said with a chuckle. "To answer your question, yes. Some people are able to communicate with the spirits in the Realm of the Dead, but that is very rare that it happens. It's rare, because in order to do so, you must have peace within your own spirit. Some people can control their spirit while awake and others only while resting. It's the reason that I desire you to meditate with me. If your spirit is not at peace or rest, you will never hear my words.

"What made you think of that question?" Emmanuel asked with a look of confusion.

"I just wanted to know. I've heard multiple times of someone being able to speak with the dead. I didn't know if this were true or if it were just a scheme of some sort."

"Well, it's not always a fact. There are perhaps more false prophets than those who have actually heard from the Heavens. An on-the-spot genuine prophecy is very unlikely. The spirit being in a state of peace and rest in that moment is rare. Nonetheless, after meditation, prayer and rest, you are more likely to hear a word from the Heavens. A man without peace is a man without direction."

"If I wanted to hear you tomorrow, could I hear you if my spirit were at peace? What I mean is, does everyone have the gift to hear you? Are we all capable?"

Emmanuel leaned forward. "George, it takes someone who is truly exceptional in order to hear the voice of God. Not only that, but dedication is also what creates and expands the gifts of everyone. If you want to be the best dancer, singer or writer, you would need to find determination and be extremely dedicated. Through God, you can achieve whatever it is that you desire to achieve as long as it is done within his will. To hear the Word of God and know that it is true, you must dedicate yourself to hearing from him. However, God will only communicate with you if he desires to do so. Sometimes, this happens regularly, and at other times it happens only when he knows you need the direction or guidance. Nonetheless, even if he doesn't give you direction when you seek it, it doesn't mean that he isn't working on a great plan for you."

Emmanuel sat back in his seat. "Did that answer your question?"

"I think so. I'm pretty satisfied," I said, nodding

my head. "Does anyone get direct access to the Heavens, or do we all have to wait until judgment?"

"Currently, the gates within the Realm of the Dead are closed and will only be opened upon my return. At that moment, it will be open for all to receive their final judgment. Once final judgment is given, Sheol, Hades and the entire Realm of the Dead besides the Abyss will be destroyed."

"Why do your followers have to wait until then?"

"Because I haven't returned to get them yet, George," Emmanuel said convincingly.

I nodded in understanding and then gazed at Emmanuel's drawing for a moment longer, realizing how it all worked. Then I asked, "Was the world created by the same energy that will one day destroy it?"

Emmanuel smirked. "So, you get that part?"

"I think I read about that somewhere. It's said that the same energy that created the Universe will one day pull the Universe back. Is that how the Earth and the Heavens will be destroyed, by the Abyss? If so, then doesn't that contradict some religions? How can a follower believe in science and in God?"

Emmanuel laughed. "Calm down, George. Do you not understand that God is the ultimate scientist and the greatest mathematician? Everything of your world is created from math and science. Through God, they all coincide to create and maintain your world. Do you believe that your brain could function if Father God didn't know how to calculate or formulate properly? You can believe in science and still believe in God. However, you need to understand that God created the science that you believe."

I sat in awe staring out in the direction of the bar

before Emmanuel interrupted. "What are you thinking about, George?"

"It's just hard for me to grasp all of this. I just always believed that God was beyond anything that man could think up."

"What do you mean?"

"I just didn't think that man could understand the workings of God. I never thought it was possible to agree with them both."

"Well, man is created in the image of God. Give yourself more credit for being created in the likes of God Almighty. In your defense, you never trained yourself to understand the workings of the world or nature. Not everyone is a scientist, physicist, biologist or even an evangelist for that matter. How everything works isn't for one person to truly understand. If you based your life solely on trying to figure out how it worked, you would never have time to figure out how to live it properly. Not just that, but the only thing that should matter is figuring out how to receive God's approval. Understanding the world is irrelevant if you don't understand God. By learning who he is, you can find appreciation in the things that you don't know. Be mindful in the things you seek to know, George. Spending too much time on one thing can lead you away from the truth of how it works in connection with everything else. Don't let your ignorance neglect truth."

"Thanks, Emmanuel. Though I'm still a bit baffled on this whole thing, I do understand it better."

Emmanuel grabbed the salt and pepper and played with them before continuing. "Because of me, through my death and resurrection, I created a bridge that connects the righteous to the Heavens. My death took me to the Realm of the Dead, and my resurrection took me to the Heavens. Because of my sacrifice, I have bridged the connection that was once lost because of sin."

"What do you mean?"

Emmanuel tried to illustrate with his hands. "Sheol expands beyond Hell. It is connected to the higher Heavens through something similar to a bridge, a bridge that was once broken because of sin. Soon, the gates from Paradise to the Heavens above will be closed permanently, and it will be no more.

I stared out the window thinking of more questions and then asked, "Which Heaven is God in and where does a normal believer go when they get to the Heavens above?"

"There are many Heavens, George. However, there are three Heavens that you should find most important. The first I taught you is Sheol. It is within the heart of the Earth, where the righteous await my return. That place is known as the Telestial Kingdom. The second Heaven is the Terrestrial Kingdom. This is where the righteous go once they have been resurrected and passed through judgment. Upon entering the second Kingdom with me, the Telestial Kingdom will be destroyed and will be no more. The third Heaven is known as the Celestial Kingdom. It is where my Father resides."

"What about the people who are already there? Are any of them in the Celestial Kingdom with God?"

"There are many spirits in the Kingdom with God. They are those who have come from Earth and are blameless according to the laws of Moses. Before me, there were many who were resurrected up to my Father to live with him in his Kingdom."

As I tried to think of another question, Emmanuel continued. "The Old Testament of your Bible was created as an order to live that would gain you access to the Heavens. Once my Father realized that humans were incapable of following the commandments and that they were nothing more than followers of man, he sent me, his Son, for them to follow. Once I came to Earth, the words of the Old Testament were voided as a way to Heaven and kept only as a story of my Father's love. I am now the only key for man to enter the Heavens above.

"Many before you have made it to Heaven not through me, but through their hearts repentance and following of the laws. Nonetheless, many more have entered the Abyss because of their disobedience.

"Your Bible was created so it could thoroughly equip you with the knowledge that you need in order to enter the Kingdom. If you live like me, then you will die like me. If you die like me, then you will be resurrected like me. Even as I died and went to the Realm of the Dead, so will you also."

"I get what you're saying. I just don't understand why it's necessary for everyone to go to the Realm of the Dead after they die."

Emmanuel took a moment before responding. "Consider this: If believers go to the high Heavens and sinners go to the Pit upon their death, then what is the value of Judgment Day, which you clearly accept? Wouldn't that mean that judgment was done upon death and that my coming would have no purpose? When I come, I'm coming to get my family. That is my purpose for coming."

Seeing my confusion, he continued. "George, believing in me only gets you a ticket to come to the Kingdom. However, I am the ride that will take you there. You must wait for me to come and pick you up."

I nodded my head in understanding. "Why is it that no one wanted to follow God? Is it just because of sin that people have chosen to reject him?"

"People don't want to believe that God exists because they don't want to be held down by rules or judgment. However, every person has knowledge of God deep within his or her heart."

I asked my next question nervously. "Who are the 144,000 I've always heard about?"

Emmanuel looked out the window and replied softly while staring at the clouds, "That is how many will come to the world in its final days and preach the final message. They will be the righteous ones who have no lie in their mouths and who are blameless to the laws. They will come in my name before and during the tribulation, and they will minister a final message to the people. They are those who will lead the people through the tribulation and save them from the Abyss."

"Are your followers going to go through the tribulation also?"

Emmanuel turned and faced me. "If you believe in me, George, then you should already be raised to the high Heavens by the time of the tribulation. The 144,000 are needed on Earth because there will be no more righteous people on Earth at the time of my coming."

"I didn't think about that," I said. "If the resurrection comes before the tribulation, then that means that all the believers will be gone. If they are gone, then someone needs to spread the message about you. Those who will do that will be the 144,000."

"That's correct, George."

"Some believe that the 144,000 are those who will be resurrected and accepted into Heaven at the end of days. Also, don't the 144,000 contradict what you said earlier about no one being righteous or sinless? Now you're telling me that there are 144,000 who are righteous and sinless."

Emmanuel laughed. "George, the 144,000 have been offered to my Father and me after their birth. They have been redeemed from Earth as newborn children, given by their Earthly parents as first fruits. Heaven has been their home since childhood, and they know nothing of their life on Earth. In addition, if only that small number of spirits were accepted from Earth during my second return, then life would be useless and limited. My Father's house doesn't have a capacity. If you believe in me, then you will be with me in Heaven. That's all there is to it."

I chuckled when I realized that through Emmanuel's teaching I was finally able to learn of the things that had boggled my thoughts for years.

Emmanuel stood up from his seat and was about to say something before I interrupted. "Who is God?"

Emmanuel thought to himself and smiled. "God is the Creator. The one who created you and all that exist. Because of him, you are, and you are because of him."

"I get that part, but how can God create everything, but not himself be created by another? It doesn't make sense how something just is. Everything comes from something. It's the law of life and of nature."

"God is God, George. There were no other gods before him."

"Tell me this: If God is your Father, then who are your grandparents?"

"George, I know it may be difficult for you to wrap your head around, but God is the beginning and the end. I know you want to believe that even he can't be perfect and complete or infinite, but he is. He doesn't exist as you may know man to exist. He was not birthed through a womb, nor will he die on Earth. Neither does he have a body full of vital organs that can be destroyed because of illness or age. You have to stop thinking of God as a man, and know him as the Spirit God that he is.

"Just know God as the uncreated Creator, the explained unexplained, the definition of definition, the Law of Law, the Holy of Holy, the Lord of Lords, and the King of Kings.

"Don't waste your time trying to create him into an inept character, but take that time to love him because he sent me to spare your life from the Pit of Hell."

Cephas walked into the room with my clean clothes in his hands. "Is it time yet?" he asked Emmanuel.

Emmanuel nodded, and then Cephas handed me the clothes. "Here you are. Please change in the bathroom and leave the extra clothes on the sink."

I thanked Cephas and then walked to the bathroom to get changed.

When I returned, Cephas was gone.

"Please take a seat and face me, George,"

Emmanuel said.

I sat down in a booth seat with my feet out to the side and looked up at him. "What's going on? What are we doing?"

Without answering my questions, Emmanuel stood up in front of me and then placed his hand over my eyes.

Eleven
A DOUBLE SHOT

The flesh of a man limits the heart of his spirit.

Emmanuel removed his hand from my eyes.

"What happened?" I asked.

Emmanuel didn't answer. "Follow me," he said.

I got up from my seat and slowly started to ascend toward the ceiling of the diner. When I realized what was going on, I panicked and tried to gain back control until I noticed that my body was still sitting in the seat, slumped over sideways.

Emmanuel looked up to me. "Come down from there," he said calmly.

I began to float back down from the ceiling. On my way down, I stared at my body there in the seat. For some reason, I felt no fear. My thoughts told me I should have been in hysteria, but the only thing I felt was freedom. It was as if I had floated out of my body and was embraced in love and peace.

"Follow me." Emmanuel began walking toward the back doors of the diner.

Without causing myself to move, I began following Emmanuel as if I were a cloud being pushed by the wind.

I lifted my hands up to my face and saw beams of small lights traveling and forming what used to be my fleshly hand. There were thousands, if not millions, of lustrous colors; colors I had neither seen nor knew existed. Not only did they mold my hands, but they were also all throughout my arms and formed my entire body. When I waved my hands, a stream of the multicolored lights flowed behind them, coloring the air. When I saw the magnificence of what I had become, I finally knew what Emmanuel meant when he said that there was spiritual energy surrounding all living things.

I focused my thoughts and tried to take back control of my spirit. When I finally did, I fell down to the floor, stood up straight and started walking. With each step I took, I left an imprint of color, as if I were walking in the mud. I turned around to look at my body once more, and when I did, I saw a streak of soft light that must have been flowing behind me the entire time. It traveled up from my body to the ceiling and followed me back down to where I was standing.

Entranced by the sight and elegance of the lights I had created, I walked backwards, watching my path without realizing where I was going. I felt a chill blanket me and then noticed a door in front of me. I turned around to look at where I was and realized that I had walked through the doors and into the next room.

I looked all around the small room before focusing my attention on Emmanuel who stood waiting. When he came near me, calmness filled my being, and I stopped moving.

He lowered his head and began whispering a prayer. When he finished, the floor beneath us pulled away, and we both fell into nothingness. Right before my eyes, I watched Emmanuel as he morphed into a human figure created of light, just as I was. However, he wasn't full of color. Instead, he was pure white, bright light that I couldn't stop myself from staring at as we continued falling.

He flew over to me, and once he grabbed my hand, our fall stopped.

I looked at Emmanuel and saw that he had the same image as he did in human form. His face and body were exactly the same, only there was no flesh covering him. His face and body had been sculpted out of light with only shadows to portray his flesh that once was.

Overwhelmed with a sense of peace and comfort, I asked calmly, "Why am I not afraid?"

Emmanuel smiled. "The mind creates the fear, not the spirit. You've been released from your worries. Because your spirit is with me, there is no more grief or fear, tears or sadness."

I looked around to my surroundings and saw only blackness. "Where are we?" I asked.

"We're within the sky of your Universe."

"Where is everything?"

Emmanuel placed one of his hands up and waved it over the sky. "Show yourself," he said.

When his hand went down, and once the streak of light flowing from it faded, I saw the stars sparkling in their position and then the lights of the planets followed. I gazed at the collage of blue, white, purple and gold lights for several minutes without saying anything. I could see planets and galaxies that appeared to have been light-years away. My vision was stronger and clearer than anything that the world could have artificially created. It was stronger than even the greatest satellites in space.

"Beautiful," I said as I continued gazing at the sparkling white speckles of light within the purple streaks of clouds that danced around me.

I turned, and through the lucent colors, my attention was drawn to a planet with mottled colors of black and white flowing on its surface. The spots were random, some small and some large in scale. Even in large black areas, there were some speckles of white and the same with speckles of black being in the large white areas. There was no pattern or flow, just randomness of black and white.

"That's the world you live in," Emmanuel said.

"That's Earth?"

"Yes," he nodded.

"Why doesn't it have any color?"

"Because you are no longer blind to the spirit world. Your spirit is no longer a hostage to your body or filtered by your mind. It has always desired more than you have allowed it. The flesh of a man limits the heart of his spirit. How you are seeing your world now is how I see it. There are no colors, only black and white; those who believe and those who don't, and those who love me and those who love against me. Spirits cover your entire world. Angels, demons and neutral spirits fill your planet."

I put my hands up to look at them. "Why am I not black or white?"

"You are. What you're seeing is how you view yourself. Because you don't know who you are, you see only chaos and confusion."

I stared at my hands. "What color do you see me as?"

Emmanuel smiled faintly. "You'll know soon enough."

Placing my attention back to the Earth, I watched and realized that the large spots that covered the planet were countries. I could easily see which countries kept God first and which were full of dark matter because of the people within them.

Once I understood the world as God did, I realized that it was such a simple planet, yet it was greater than the world I knew.

I contemplated how small the Earth was compared to the entire Universe. I had always known that there were billions of other planets, but I never realized until that moment how mere the world was in comparison. All of the problems I had or bitter feelings toward those I was in a relationship with seemed more insignificant than ever. My existence had only become a black or white speckle on such a massive scale. The only thing that truly mattered was if I loved God. In his black and white world, there were no rainbows of excuses. Either you belonged to the light or you fell into the shadows of darkness.

"How did this happen?" I asked. "How did the world come to be like this? Why did God send Satan to Earth knowing we would be there? If we just loved God like we should have from the beginning, the Earth would be another shining star in his eyes."

Emmanuel replied, "God didn't send Satan to Earth, George. Satan only had access to the Earth and to the Heavens, just as all angels in the beginning.

"The first humans were on Earth with God, Satan

and many other angels. However, once sin came upon the Earth, God closed the gates to Heaven and left sin to roam the Earth. That meant that humans, Satan and his followers were left here together. The design wasn't to send evil to Earth by way of Satan. It was to create Earth as another Heaven, allowing angels to go to and from as they pleased. A sinless Heaven could not remain open to a sinful Earth. Because of sin, Earth had to be somewhat quarantined to keep sin from traveling to Heaven. Through believing and following me, I will cleanse you from sin and allow you back into Heaven."

When Emmanuel finished speaking, I knew I had finally understood everything he had been trying to explain to me. When I thought about it, I connected my understanding to the fact that I had been in the spirit form. Without the distractions of my mind, I could easily interpret Emmanuel's message. When Emmanuel said I needed to let my spirit take control so that I could hear him, I never knew what it meant until that moment.

I gazed at Emmanuel, and joy comforted me as I began to fall in love. The love I felt for him was much greater than anything that I had ever felt for Carol and Mindy. I didn't love him just because of who he was today, but also because of who he was yesterday and who he will be tomorrow. I realized then that Emmanuel loved me before I was even a thought in my mother's womb. Even when I didn't love myself, he knew me and loved me deeper than I ever knew. The love I experienced for him wasn't just a feeling, but it healed me. All I wanted to do at that moment was praise him and thank him for allowing me to choose the life I was undeservingly given.

When I finally pulled myself from staring at Emmanuel, I turned back and looked at the Earth. I watched what seemed to be some sort of battle being fought for the soul of man.

"Can a man be possessed by a spirit?" I asked.

Emmanuel continued watching the Earth. "Demons can only possess a man with his permission. Unfortunately, man is fooled into giving this consent because demons are kings of deceit. Even so, a demon can only possess a man's body and mind, but not his spirit. The spirit of man protects the Holy Spirit within him. Because the Holy Spirit is the piece of man that is created in God's image, a demon can never control it. What the demon does instead is control your mind. If it can control your mind, then it can manipulate your spirit. By empowering your spirit and making it holy, you can maintain control of your mind through God's knowledge, thereby fending off demons who try to enter it."

Emmanuel took one of my hands and led me as we began soaring through space at lightning speed toward the Earth. Just as we entered the atmosphere of the planet, a bright light appeared and created a tunnel. We traveled through the colorful warped tunnel for only a few seconds before we entered an immense open area of white space. We slowed and floated downward until we reached a hard surface. I took a few steps and noticed that the lights of my footsteps where gone. When I put my hands up to look at them, I no longer saw lights, but only flesh.

"What happened? Am I still in the spirit?" I looked up at Emmanuel and saw that his flesh had also returned.

"Yes, George. You are in the spirit. However, you

are now in Sheol. You see things differently here. You see what you have become used to, the things that bring you comfort."

I looked around Sheol and could see nothing but white light, with the exception of Emmanuel and me. The light of Sheol covered me with a sensation of love and healing. It embraced and warmed me as I found delight in its ambience. I stood with my eyes closed and breathed in its coveted energy.

As I relaxed, I asked Emmanuel, "Is this Paradise and the first Heaven?"

Emmanuel nodded.

I looked around. "Where is everyone?"

"You haven't created them yet," Emmanuel answered.

I turned and looked at him in wonder. "What do you mean?"

Emmanuel smiled. "Sheol is like a sweet dream of Paradise. Like a dream, Sheol takes your most-loved memories and thoughts and transforms them into comfort.

"In the first Heaven, you see what your spirit loves most. You also see the spirits of those who love and have loved you. You may see your wife, daughter, parents, pet or even me or my Father. You may even see the spirit of a current loved one who is still living. In Sheol, you create your paradise."

As Emmanuel finished speaking, I looked around and saw hills of grass and flowers surrounding me. I closed and then opened my eyes and noticed a beach, water and sand right in front of me. I walked over and placed my foot into the water.

"Is this real?" I smiled, as the energy of the warm water flowed throughout my body

"It's as real as you believe it to be."

I ran along a thin strip of the water with my hands up in the air, feeling the force of the ocean breeze through my fingers. When I finished running, I was filled with the pure joy of contentment. I sat down in the sand and laughed when I realized that I wasn't tired or thirsty after the long run. Normally, I would have fallen because of exhaustion, but in Paradise, I was full of energy and life.

I looked back in the direction in which I came and saw Emmanuel walking over to me. When I saw who was with him, I leaped up and starting running toward them. Joy filled me, and I stretched my arms wide preparing to wrap them around Carol, Mindy and Addison who were running toward me with huge smiles on their faces.

I closed my eyes and held my family in my arms until Emmanuel walked behind me and placed his hand on my shoulder. I turned to look at him for just a moment, but when my gaze returned to my family, they had become images fading into nothingness. I looked around and saw that the fields of grass and beach had also vanished. It was again just Emmanuel and I.

"What's going on?" I asked.

"That was only a preview, George. We have to continue our journey."

Enchanted by my love for Emmanuel, I trusted and followed him without questioning where he was taking me.

Emmanuel and I started walking toward nothing in particular until I asked, "If there are billions of spirits here, then where are they?"

Emmanuel stopped walking and faced me. Placing

his hand over my eyes, he said a prayer. When he let go, I looked around and instead of seeing fields of grass or white light; I saw human spirits kneeling with their heads down before Emmanuel. Instead of the sky and ground being bright and white, it was a blue color that almost matched the atmosphere of the Earth. The spirits near the surface of the ground looked like clouds hovering. I looked in front of Emmanuel, saw a clear path left between the billions of spirits and realized that Emmanuel was following it.

I knelt down to look closer at one of the spirits and instead of flesh or colors; it was filled with the same white light as Emmanuel. I stood up and looked at all of the spirits. Each had no hair and a white robe covering their body.

I again looked closer and saw only blurred faces of no real form and could see no gender, race, height, weight or age amongst any of the spirits. When I looked at my own hands and body, I again saw millions of moving colors traveling through me.

Emmanuel walked over to me and placed his hand back over my eyes before saying another prayer. This time when I opened them, the spirits were gone and I could only see Emmanuel.

We started walking again, and I stayed close behind him, knowing that following him would keep me from stepping on anyone. I knew that with Emmanuel, I didn't need to see where we were going; I only needed to follow his lead. He knew the way, and I made sure not to question where he placed his feet.

Emmanuel continued to walk straight, and I could hear him snickering each time I corrected myself after

I got off track.

"Why did they all look the same?" I asked Emmanuel.

He answered while continuing to walk. "A spirit never ages. Only the mind and body age. The spirit is the same from the beginning of your life until its end. It was created in the image of God, and what you've seen here is that image. Everyone is equal, and all souls are alike in design."

"Are we inside of the Earth?"

"Yes."

"Why is it so bright in here then?"

"Do you know anything about what your planet is made of?" Emmanuel asked.

"Yes. I know some."

"The Earth's inner layers are created from a fiery substance just as the sun. Like the sun that brightens Earth's sky, the light of the world covers Sheol. The sky of Sheol is the same as the sky of the Earth. Sheol is the Earth below the Earth. However, Sheol has a stronger protection from its sun, and the spirit can withstand the radiation of the light. The reason I didn't transform until after you were out of your body is because your flesh wouldn't have been able to endure the light of who I am."

I looked around. "I just always pictured the inside of the Earth to be dark and gloomy. Because it's surrounded by darkness, I thought the inside would be the same or at least affected by it."

Emmanuel turned to face me. "George, your planet is also covered by nothing but darkness. However, it still shines because of the sun. Just as the sun lights the Earth, so does the light of the world cover Sheol," he said before turning around and continuing to walk.

We walked for what felt like almost an hour before Emmanuel stopped in front of me. He turned around. "We're here."

I looked up and around and saw nothing. "Where are we?"

Emmanuel turned to me again and instead of placing his hand on my eyes, he placed it on my forehead and began praying.

When I opened my eyes, there stood a massive mountainous structure. The dark structure stretched left and right beyond what I could see and angled up, reaching above the atmospheric sky.

When I looked down, I had realized why Emmanuel had stopped walking. We had arrived at a river created of a flowing, lava-like substance. Looking across the river, I saw that the entire ground and mountain structure in front of us was also made of the same substance. Continuing to observe the structure, I recognized that it was an enormous volcano covered in darkened volcanic rock.

"Are we going over there?" I asked Emmanuel.

He nodded.

Immediately after his nod, we were across the lake. I twirled around, confused about how we arrived across the river without walking. "How did we get here?" I asked.

"I thought us here," Emmanuel said calmly.

"You can think of places and then go?"

"Yes, George. With the Holy Spirit, you can travel also by the speed of thought. It is how God created the world you live in today."

"Why didn't we just do that to get here? We just walked for over an hour. Couldn't you have just thought us here?"

"I could have, but my family wanted to see me, and I wanted to see them. There was no rush to make it here."

Still amazed at what just happened, I stood in awe and stared back out across the river into the light on the other side.

As I remembered Emmanuel's drawing of the Realm of the Dead, I finally understood where we were.

"Is this Hell?" I said anxiously.

"Yes," Emmanuel said before looking up to the sky near the structure. "Leave here!" he shouted toward the sky and then looked away.

I didn't ask what he shouted at. I was only concerned by the fact that I had been in fear.

"I thought you said that if I were in the spirit, my feelings would cease to exist."

"Only in Sheol, George. In Hell, you feel everything that your flesh would also feel. In Hell, you are in the spirit, but you gain back the consciousness of your mind."

I looked up at the tall structure. "I don't think I ever believed this place existed before now."

"You are like many, George. There are many who believe in the existence of Heaven, but not in the existence of Hell."

"Is Satan in there?" I asked, as we were about 50 yards away from the gates of the structure.

"Satan isn't in there, George."

"Where is he then?" I asked, nervously afraid of what might be inside the dark mountain.

"Satan is roaming the Earth. He has been here, and he comes whenever he chooses, as God allows him to roam the entire Earth."

"What you were looking at in the sky, was that Satan?"

Emmanuel nodded his head to confirm.

A sense of relief came over me as I realized I had the protection of Emmanuel. I didn't know where we were going, but I did know that as long as I had Emmanuel I would be safe from anything.

"Is Satan the ruler of Hell?" I asked.

"Not at all, George. Satan isn't the ruler of anything. He is only a prisoner of this world. He doesn't desire to be here, just as no spirit does.

"Are there other demons here?"

"Yes, he does recruit other demons. However, Lucifer does not love souls, as they are God's creations. He hates the fact that he is here on Earth living in a world in which God constructed."

I walked close and cautiously behind Emmanuel. "Are there also spirits in here that I can't see?"

"There are many spirits here."

"Are they kneeling also, or are they looking at us?" I asked timidly.

"They are also kneeling. However, instead of kneeling in joy, they bow their heads in shame."

"What are they doing here? I thought you said that the prison for the unrighteous was in Hades."

"It is. This is only the waiting place before they continue to Hades. This is where death first takes them. If these spirits would have simply believed in me, they would have found refuge in death instead of being sent to this place.

"What you don't see is the formation of spirits waiting at the entrance. You don't hear the crying or see the tears. Unlike Sheol, in Hell you see what your mind fears most. In Hell, you are who you were before Hell. This is a place not of smiles, laughter and joy, but of fear and torment.

"Hell doesn't quench a man's soul. It only enhances its dismay. Once these spirits walk into Hades, they'll see and experience things they have never imagined. In Hades, they will yearn for their worst fears, as they will know things that are much worse."

"Is what they did so bad that they have to suffer through this?"

Emmanuel stopped walking and looked at me. "It was easy, George. It was very easy to believe in me. However, many don't believe until they encounter death. They have their entire lifetime to choose. I only asked them to believe in me. However, these spirits live in anger. They lie, steal, cheat and curse my name. They are bitter, unforgiving and sexually immoral. I have told you many times that those who do such things shall not inherit the Kingdom of God. The reason they have no peace is because they refused it when it was offered."

Emmanuel and I continued walking, and when we approached the gate that surrounded the massive mountain, the doors screeched open. We walked carefully on the smooth rock and up to one of the many arched entrances of Hades.

We stepped into the large structure, and immediately I smelled a stench greater than anything I could have imagined. The foul smell nearly caused me to fall over as I struggled to catch my breath. I covered my nose, but the odor didn't cease, it only bled through the cracks of my fingers and seeped through the pores of my flesh.

Hades was pitch black and filled with nothing but gloomy darkness. I grabbed onto Emmanuel's clothing and walked carefully behind him.

When we had gone far enough into Hades, Emmanuel stopped, said a prayer and transformed himself back into spirit form. The light that projected from him lit the way as we continued to walk down a long tunnel with small prison-like rooms, or cages, on each side. There were hundreds of thousands of cages we passed. They not only surrounded us left and right, but they were everywhere, stacked on top of one another reaching higher than I could see as if they were boxes in a warehouse.

Afraid, I remained close to Emmanuel, but I was also able to follow his footsteps that were left behind from his spirit.

I had never been more terrified in my life. I could only imagine what types of demons were surrounding me in those cages. The cages were endless in number. As we walked, I saw many more tunnels to the right and left of me, all lined with more cages. I only hoped that we would hurry and do whatever it was that we came to do.

"Are there people in those cages?"

"Yes," Emmanuel answered as we continued to walk.

We had been walking through that long tunnel for what felt like two hours. I wanted to ask Emmanuel why he wouldn't just travel by thought, but I figured he had his reasons.

The stench of Hades didn't diminish, either. I had to force myself to breathe as I occasionally gasped for air.

After another hour of walking, we finally stopped,

and Emmanuel looked down in front of him.

"We're here," he said.

I stepped to the side of him, looked down and noticed a large manhole-type cover on the floor. Smoke was coming up from its cracks and was steaming the entire area where we stood. Through Emmanuel's light, I could see that the lid must have been about 50 feet in diameter with a crack down the middle, as if it were a door.

Next to Emmanuel's foot, I saw some etching on the side of the lid. I knelt down to see if I could read what it said. After removing the dirt from the writing, I read, "*Ge'enna.*"

"What does this mean?" I asked.

"It's the place where the fire will not be quenched."

"Is this the lake of fire?"

Emmanuel nodded.

I stood up in shock after realizing where we were. I began to gasp even harder for air and had to kneel back down in order to maintain composure.

I remained knelt down and asked Emmanuel, "why is the Pit so small? I thought it would be like a real lake."

"This opening is only that—an opening. The Pit is beneath it. The Lake stretches from here to the outside of Hell." Emmanuel knelt down next to me. "Beneath this surface, there are billions of spirits burning in the Lake of Fire. These are the spirits of those who have already been judged. Upon my second judgment, this Pit will be opened, and those who have denied me will be thrown into the fiery furnace for all of eternity."

Emmanuel and I both knelt down. He placed his

hand on my shoulder and started to pray.

When his hand left me, I looked up and heard loud screams and crying in a language I could not comprehend. The sounds filled my ears, and I closed my eyes and covered them, hoping that it would stop. The noises were coming from all around.

I looked at Emmanuel and cried, "Why are you doing this? Make it stop, please!"

The light from Emmanuel grew and showed me all that was in the large circular room. Through the smoke, I could see demons everywhere. Not human demons, but dark beasts with broken wings. The creatures stood hunched over, staring at me while I held close to Emmanuel for security. They stood all around us, growling and gnashing their teeth.

I continued to look beyond them and could see men and women in human form fighting against chains and kicking on the bars that were holding them hostage in the cages. They screamed and wailed endlessly. Some cursed at Emmanuel, and others cried out for his help.

I stayed close to Emmanuel's protection and pleaded for him to stop the pain.

Without saying anything, he turned around and started walking back in the direction in which we came.

As we traveled down the long tunnel, the demons with wings followed us, getting as close as they could without going into Emmanuel's light.

The spirits in the cages continued screaming, and their crying worsened as they surrounded us. They began calling out my name and those who were unchained stretched their hands out toward me.

"How do they know me? Please stop this! Please!"

Emmanuel just continued walking and ignored everything I said.

Another spirit in a prison called my name, and I turned to him. I could see the morbid beast that he was. Maggots covered his body where the rough skin had been ripped in several places. They were feeding on his open wounds. The demon had sharp teeth and nails, and he placed his hands between the bars, directing me to come toward him. I fought myself to stop looking, as it had become difficult to do so. I looked around at all of the cages and became overwhelmed with the loud screaming and chains slamming against the prison bars. All of the suffering on Earth was nothing compared to Hades. It was everything I feared all in one place. When I couldn't take it any longer, I grabbed Emmanuel's arm, forcing him to stop.

"Release me, child of Lucifer!" Emmanuel exclaimed as he turned around, grabbed my hand and threw it away from him.

Twelve
ADD THE CREAM

The fact that I don't deserve forgiveness is the true beauty of God's grace.

Shock and confused, I stared at Emmanuel, not understanding his hostile demeanor toward me. "Please! What have I done?"

My ears began to bleed as the screams and growls of the prisoners of Hades grew louder. Falling down to my knees, I begged and pleaded for Emmanuel to save my life and release the pain.

Emmanuel looked down upon me. "You are no follower of mine."

When he spoke, the prisoners in Hades grew quiet and allowed his voice to easily project over their own.

Tears welled up in my eyes. "Please, Jesus! What have I done, Lord? Why would you leave me like this?"

"Now you call me *Jesus* and *Lord?* You have sinned against me, cursed my name and called my teachings a lie. Now you want to call me your God?"

I fell to my face. “Please, let me speak with God so that I may explain. Please, he will understand.”

Emmanuel backed away from me, and the shield of his light moved with him. Trying to stay out of the light, the demons grabbed for my legs. I kicked and screamed until I was able to crawl back into Emmanuel’s light for protection.

Emmanuel continued. “My Father will never accept you without my approval. Your voice is deaf to his ears. Your words are sour, and your spirit is infected. You will never make it to the Heavens above to speak with my Father, nor will he come down to Hades to relieve you from your suffering. You have made your choice. You have chosen yourself to be your false god. My Father is not a son of man that he shall speak and not abide by his own words. Nor does he promise and not fulfill, or change his mind. By denying me, you have sinned against him and made your choice. Therefore, he has also made his.”

“Why, Jesus? You told me that I wasn't dead. Why have you lied to me?”

“I never said such a thing. I only said that you were alive. A spirit never dies. You twist my words and hear what you desire to hear. You have wasted your time by lacking knowledge and direction. You place words in my mouth to satisfy your comforts. I have had to prove myself repeatedly to you, and you still haven't learned. How insignificant am I to you that I need endless proof for you to love me?”

Emmanuel continued to speak, and with each word, he backed up farther down the tunnel as I crawled toward him trying to stay within his light.

Tears flowed from my eyes and pooled on the floor of the prison. I crawled, begging, “I don’t know what to do. Please, I need another chance. I didn't have good direction. There was no one there for me to follow. I tried, but no one taught me how to truly believe. Please Jesus, I'll do better."

Emmanuel stopped moving backwards, closed his eyes and then began crying.

I held back my pain when I looked up and saw his tears. As he cried, I realized that he was suffering worse than I was. He didn't desire for me to go to Hades. He was losing someone he loved, just as I had when I lost my family.

Sorrow and pity filled his voice as he turned to me and said, "It's too late."

Just then, I heard the voices of Carol and Mindy coming from behind me. When I turned to look in the direction of the voices, the light of Emmanuel faded, and I was left with nothing but total darkness.

Silence filled Hades, and I could hear only my own heavy breathing. Crawling backwards in fear, I hoped that the room was empty. I began to stand up, but the demons grabbed my legs and started pulling me back down the tunnel. The more I tried to fight against them, the harder their sharp claws dug into my flesh as they held on tightly. The clanking chains, screams and gnashing teeth of the prisoners grew louder as I yelled incessantly for Jesus, but the demons kept dragging me across the rugged floor of Hades.

I closed my eyes and cried out, "No! Jesus, please! Don't leave me!"

The demons stopped dragging me, and a loud bang rang out, followed by complete silence.

"George! George! Can you hear me?" someone

shouted.

"Please! No!" I screamed wailing my arms and legs.

"George! Open the door."

When I realized that my legs weren't being held, I apprehensively opened one of my eyes. Through my blurred vision and tears, I saw the inside of the sports car that Steve and I had rented.

"George!"

I looked around the inside of the car, paranoid and trying to see where the voice was coming from.

"George! Open up."

Turning to the window next to me, I saw Steve knocking on the glass and calling my name. I wiped the tears from my eyes and then rolled down the window.

Still shaking because of the terrifying experience, I tried to stay calm as I spoke to Steve. "What's up, Steve?"

"Hey man, I got you back into the meeting. I talked with thc Bishop and told him what was going on. They said you can come in and finish your presentation," Steve said eagerly. He then looked at me and a puzzled look came over his face. "Are you okay? Your eyes are red."

"I'm fine, I'm okay. I was just sleeping."

"You were only out here for five minutes. How did you fall asleep so quickly? Anyway, are you coming in?"

"No, I'm okay waiting."

"Are you serious? What am I supposed to tell them? I just wasted my meeting time building you up and now you act as if you don't care."

"I'm fine here, Steve. Please."

Steve shook his head in disappointment. "Just wait in the car then," he said before running back into the building.

After I watched him go back into the church, tears welled up in my eyes and flooded down my face. Cradling myself, I cried like a small child while remembering the dream that had turned into a nightmare.

I looked over to the passenger seat at my briefcase. I opened it and took out my Bible. Wrapping my hands around it and holding it to my chest, I began praying. "God," I said, looking up to the roof of the car. "I love you deeply. More than I ever have. Of the billions of people who talk to you every day, you found me worthy and special enough to meet and walk with you."

Calming myself, I put my head down and reflected on the goodness of the experience. When I remembered the beautiful memories with Emmanuel and Cephas, I smiled knowing that it was all for a greater purpose. Instead of crying, I thought of Cephas and what he would ask about the journey. I laughed as I could hear his interrogating voice questioning, "*What have you learned?*"

I got out of the car and placed my elbows on the roof. Looking up to the sky and seeing the shining stars, I felt the peace of God cover me as I began praying. "God, I've learned that you are easier than anything I know. I've lived for the love of myself for many years. I never truly gave you enough thanks and praise."

I paused and thought about my life before continuing my prayer. "The reality is that I asked for much more than I ever gave thanks for. I can't ever say that I truly believed in you. I was only addicted to the habit of saying it. Even so, if I do believe in you, I know now that it's not enough to just say it. Believing means nothing without the action of following. I know for certain that I was never your follower. I believed in everything that you did. I believed that you were power. I knew that you were God, but I never followed you. I only watched you as you did it all, and I sat back and observed from a distance. I never cared to step out of my comfort zone and let you lead me.

"To love you doesn't mean that I can sit around and do nothing. To show someone that you love them, you must also love to do for them. I never did much of anything for you. Even when I did, I always expected something back in return. To love with an agenda means to not love at all. You have loved me even when I sinned against you."

My voice began cracking as I realized the many mistakes I had made in my life. "I thought that waking up and going to church or going to help churches was enough to get me into Heaven. I thought that by saying your name it would be enough. I thought that because I didn't curse, fight or do drugs, I would make my way into Heaven with ease. I felt that if I loved and respected the things that you love, then you would love me better. I thought that because I didn't sin actively, then by default I would be allowed into your good grace. I ignored your desires and followed only my own comforts. I never knew you for myself. I never knew your love personally."

Tears fell again as I continued. "Father God, I thank you for allowing me another day. I thank you for keeping my family safe within your light. Today, I love you more than I ever have. You are truly a loving God, and I give my life to you. In the name of Jesus my Lord, I thank you for the lessons you have honored me with.

"Please forgive me. Forgive me for my mistakes and my wrongdoings. Forgive me for not loving you as you deserve to be loved. I am weak without you. I need you God. I need you more than anything. Please accept me back into your good grace and family."

After I finished praying and was back in the car, Steve came and knocked on the window. I rolled it down, and we stared at each other a moment before I asked, "Are you done?"

"You driving or do you want me to?" Steve asked, seemingly upset.

"You can drive." I said, opening the door and getting out of the driver's seat.

Steve placed his briefcase in the back seat, and I did the same before getting into the passenger seat.

We didn't say anything to one another at first. Feeling uncomfortable and not knowing if Steve was upset with me, I asked, "How'd it go?"

He shrugged. "It was okay. I don't know."

"I didn't mess up anything, did I?"

"You sure didn't make it better. Good luck getting your job back."

The rest of the car ride was filled with silence. When we arrived back at the hotel, Steve and I went to our rooms without saying anything to one another.

Knowing how upset he was, and because I knew I had no reason to stay, I called a taxi and went to the airport to try and get on a standby flight.

I was able to get a seat on an early a.m. flight. I

arrived back in Virginia the next day around 8 a.m.

Getting into my car, I knew I didn't want to go back home. I hadn't completely gotten over Carol and Mindy being gone, and I didn't want to walk into that empty house alone. I sat in my car and cried for almost an hour before realizing what I needed to do in order to find peace and acceptance of their deaths.

I turned on my car and began driving until I arrived at the cemetery. Nervously, I got out of the car and leaned up against it. I caught my breath and tried to relax my heart, which was nearly beating out of my chest. After calming myself, I walked across the soft green grass and arrived at Carol's grave. A multitude of flowers had been placed up against her gravestone. I looked over to Mindy's and noticed the same. I figured they were probably from Carol's parents or my own.

The site of the grave and the reality of their death filled me with intense discomfort. I inhaled and exhaled deeply, hoping to keep myself from crying. As I gained composure, I opened my mouth and began speaking, trying to find any words to say.

"I've been fighting for no reason, Carol. Jesus already fought my battles, and I've spent most of my life still fighting for something that was already mine. I've been fighting for work, for direction, for purpose, and to be a good father and man. All of that was for nothing. The only thing I should have been fighting for was the love of God.

"I don't like that you're gone. However, I know that sometimes it is only during a crisis that we realize how little we know about others and ourselves. God showed me what I needed to see. Somehow, he found me worthy enough to be in his presence. The things he showed me and taught me have saved my life, and I need to make sure I find purpose out of that experience."

As I remembered everything that happened the night of the shooting, I cried deeply and painfully. "I'm really a lucky man to have had you in my life. You have no idea how much of a better man you've made me. Through your life I found happiness, and through your death I found peace. I know you are safe and happy with Mindy and Addison in Heaven, and I can assure you that I'm going to move on. I hope that I'm a changed man, Carol. I pray to God that I am good enough and pleasing to him. I know I'm unworthy and undeserving. I had God all wrong, and I'm ashamed to ever say that I didn't love him as he deserves to be loved. To love is the simplest thing that anyone can ask of me. If I love him, then everything else is as easy as remembering my love for him. The fact that I don't deserve forgiveness is the true beauty of God's grace.

"I know that I need to love God with all that I have. Love means everything. I'm going to commit myself to his desires and purpose for me. Through him, I now understand peace and true happiness at its greatest. I have to surrender what I am, in order to position myself for what I am to become. I know he has something great for me. No one else can save me, and I can't save myself. Only through God can I be saved from the Pit of Hades.

"I know you're happy and safe now with Mindy and Addison. I can't be upset. You're in a better place and I know that personally. I really do love and miss you, Carol. However, I know that I have to move on and do my part in order to get there with you."

I placed my head down on Carol's gravestone. As I pushed myself to stop crying, I smelled a faint aroma that filled my nostrils and grabbed my attention away from my sadness.

Trying to figure out what the familiar smell was, I looked around before focusing my attention on Mindy's grave. There I saw something white shining through the petals of the orchids.

I went over and moved the flowers until I uncovered a cup of cappuccino and a folded piece of paper duct-taped onto it.

I smiled and then picked up the cup. As I lifted it to my face, I saw that it was broken into many pieces and then glued back together. I then pulled the paper off the cup and unfolded it. I laughed loudly when I realized what it was. On one side of the paper was the circle that Emmanuel drew, and on the other side was the maze that he highlighted.

I reached into my pants pocket and took out a pen. After flattening the creases on the maze, I filled it in from start to finish while carefully following the path of light provided by Emmanuel.

ACKNOWLEDGEMENTS

Writing The Barista has taken over six years of research and study. The development of this novel has taken four years of editing and revisions. It simply would not have been possible without the help of many people. I first want to thank my father God for gifting me with the knowledge and wisdom. I also want to thank my wife Anastasia for putting up with my long nights of writing and for providing her valuable and loving feedback. I would also like to thank Kristy Borowik along with Fran and John Sells for their professional services.

In addition, I want to extend a heartfelt thanks to Robert and Evelena Dawson of Elkridge, Maryland, Darryl Manco of La Quinta, California, Eddie Norwood of Wake Forest, North Carolina and to Pastor Leretta C. Pettyjohn of New Beginnings Family Worship Center in Milford, Delaware for their reactions and suggestions.

To my spiritual family that has helped with my development and understanding of Christ:

New Beginnings International Christian Center in Okinawa, Japan— Through your ministries and life courses is where I first found true love and peace.

The Potter's House in Pittsburgh, Pennsylvania— Because of you I have grown a true understanding of personal purpose and position.

The Potter's House in Dallas, Texas— Here is where

I discovered motivation that taught me how to use my gifts for my purpose.

There are also many book authors, television, play and film directors and of course family and friends who have inspired me through their stories and presence.

The Barista is truly a collaborative labor.

Visit me on the web.

www.TheBaristaBook.com